Prequel Novella

The Forbidden

"When defying the gods, nowhere is safe…"

L. F. Holmes

Sign up for the author's New Releases mailing list and get a free sneak peek at the prologue of *ANCESTORS,* the first novel in the Ancestors Saga.

Visit my website to continue your journey:

www.leholmes.com/ancestors-chapter-download

To my husband, Matt, without whom none of this would have been possible.

Contents

Chapter One

Escape

The woman scrambled over the rocks of the escarpment. She had climbed far and was exhausted. Reaching the top, she glanced back once at the blood bath far below. Her eyes scoured the bloodstained snow, searching for life among the mauled forms strewn about the frosty plain.

The carnage stretched away to the thickly wooded foothills of the mighty mountain range behind. Her heart wailed when she saw no survivors. Only their savage enemies sauntered about the killing field, huge, grotesque forms spearing the fallen, seemingly for the fun of it. One by one, they began to disappear back into their mountain forest lair. Some dragged the bodies of the dead behind them, painting streaks of red across the snow.

Rebaa turned her face away, forcing down a wave of nausea. She grasped at the icy rocks surrounding her to steady herself. He was not coming. He had gotten her to safety and told her to run. He had promised he would follow.

She remembered his green eyes, filled with a mix of fear and determination. She panted, fighting back despair. Her eyes scanned the way behind her again and again but it was empty. The snow swirled in the void, cold and lifeless. He had lied. He had never intended to follow her. She should have known he would never leave the tribe at the mercy of the enemy he had awakened.

He was dead. She did not have to reach out with her higher senses to know that but some masochistic part of herself did so all the same. The nothingness that came whipping back to her was crippling. She screamed her loss to the frozen, uncaring sky.

Rebaa did not know how long she crouched there, lost in her grief, until a kick in her belly roused her. Her baby knew something was wrong and grew restless. Fresh tears leaked down her cheeks, stinging in the biting cold. What was she to do? Juran had taken her from her home, made her live among her enemies and given her his child. Now he was dead, leaving Rebaa alone and utterly defenceless. A pregnant Achalaja female far from her native land with no tribe to protect her. She was close to her time. She needed a people or she and her unborn would die. Her large indigo eyes cast about helplessly over the strange and empty lands as the wind whipped her dark hair across her fine features.

An idea flitted unbidden through her mind and she shuddered away from it. No. They would never accept her back. Her hands went to her belly. They would never understand. She dropped her head into her hands. One impossible choice after another chased its way through her thoughts. Would they kill her if she returned? Maybe. But Rebaa knew one thing for certain, she could not stay here. If she did, she was surely dead. Already, she could feel the cold seeping into her small body. Her pale red-gold skin prickled. The heavy fur wrappings were not enough to protect her out here. She had no choice. She would have to go back.

With one last despairing look at the destruction below, Rebaa heaved herself to her feet. Her mouth set into a grim line. He was not coming. She had to accept that. The life she had come to know was gone. She was at Achala's mercy now.

Turning to the empty wilderness, she walked away, leaving a piece of her heart behind her forever.

Chapter Two

Hunted

Rebaa trudged numbly through the drifting snow, stumbling and slipping often on the rock-strewn ground of the forsaken foothills fringing the great mountain range. She did not know where she was going and at times she was so consumed by grief that she did not care. Only a strange compulsion to keep moving and to return to her own people drew her on. She did not understand that. She was an outcast now. Tainted. They would drive her away as soon as they saw her. As soon as they saw-

Rebaa choked and wrapped her arms protectively round her swollen belly. Her precious one. There was nowhere she could take him where he would be safe. The only safety had been butchered far behind them. Not for the first time, her knees almost buckled under the enormity of what had happened and what she now faced. The grief and longing she felt for Juran was now overshadowed by a terrible anger at him. Tremors rolled through her body at the memory of their enemies. He should not have provoked them! He had drawn them out of their lairs and brought death upon their heads. He had forfeited the life of their child.

Rebaa cursed the moment she had ever laid eyes on him. He had entrapped her, made her live a life she hated and burdened her with a Forbidden child. He had ruined her and all she believed in. Worst of all, he had made her fall in love with him.

A sob escaped her throat. She had fought it. Achala Herself forbade such a thing but, in the end, she had not been able to help herself. She had loved Juran with all of her heart.

The cold wind blew, whistling through the rocky landscape and the sparse trees. Rebaa wrapped her dirty furs more tightly around her. She marvelled at how what had once seemed so alien was now so natural to her. Her own forest people did not wear furs. When Juran had first made her wear them, her skin had crawled with revulsion. Now her very survival depended on them.

How strange her life had become.

Despite the thick coverings, her feet were numb. She found herself stumbling more and more often. Rebaa knew she was close to exhaustion. She had been walking all day and had travelled far. She had not eaten and her baby was quiet. A new concern gnawed at her. How was she to feed herself? She was Achalaja. She did not hunt. She had felt the same way about eating meat as she had about wearing furs. It was not the Achalaja way. Her people relied on their sacred forests to feed and clothe them. Fruits, fungi, nuts, roots. That was the extent of an Achalaja diet. The great Achala had taught them to live so.

Rebaa looked to the bare, scraggly trees dotting the darkening landscape, the snow piling up about their roots. Her heart sank. These trees would not sustain her through the winter. Their bounty had long ago perished with the first frosts.

If she had been living with her people, she would have gathered provisions to see her and her tribe through the long Fury. The Cro had no such tradition. How foolish they were. How foolish she had been.

The Achalaja woman passed a hand over her eyes, fighting the weariness that was seeping into her very bones. It begged her to lay down and simply close her eyes. Rebaa shook her head sharply to clear it. She must not succumb. If she did, she would fall into a sleep from which she would never wake. She had to find shelter from the elements or she would not last the night. She shuddered. To be in such an open space was still unnerving to her. She felt horribly naked.

To her left, the low mountains rose starkly in the growing darkness, the cruel wind rolled down from their jagged heights to bite at her cheeks. To her right, great snowy plains stretched as far as the eye could see. No shelter would be found that way. She turned reluctantly into the wind.

As luck would have it, she did not have to climb far before she stumbled across the cave. It loomed out of the darkness, carved deep into a sheer wall of rock. Its black mouth yawned in the swirling snow, offering salvation. Despite all her numerous sins, Achala must still be watching out for her.

Nevertheless, shivering and on the point of collapse, Rebaa hesitated. The cave was indeed a blessing but survival instinct held her in place. Suppose something else had already made this place home? Something just as hungry as she was who wouldn't mind a snack wandering so willingly into its den in the dead of winter.

She could not see very far into the shadowy depths. Her sight had always been weak in comparison to Juran's. His eyes had been able to pick out antelope at dusk on a far horizon. No matter. She was still Achalaja and she did not need to rely on sight to know what was around her. Gathering her senses, Rebaa tasted the energies of her surroundings. Achala, in her endless wisdom, had made her people a part of the Great Spirit of the earth. His energy was hers and she only had to reach out to tap into it. Closing her eyes, she stretched out with her higher senses into the cave before her.

Nothing. The cave was empty. Relieved beyond words, Rebaa stumbled at last into its sheltering embrace. It was narrow, craggy and wound back a fair way into the rock face. It smelled of cold, damp rocks but no animal scents came to her. She ventured further inside. It was warmer in here out of the cruelty of the wind and the blanketing snow. It would be enough. Spent, she sank to the rocky floor, resting her back into an alcove where the wall was smoother. She could go no further tonight.

Tired as she was, sleep did not come immediately. Now she had stopped, the silence was oppressive. It was quiet. Far too quiet. Somewhere deeper inside the cave, water dripped from the damp ceiling into an unseen pool below. The sound echoed back and forth dimly from the surrounding rocks. Besides the whistling of the wind outside and the beating of her own heart, there was no other sound.

The dark emptiness closed in about her. She had longed for rest but now Rebaa wished she could have carried on trudging all through the night. At least when she was walking, the concentration needed to keep putting one foot in front of the other had been a distraction. Now, in the silence of this cave, the sense of isolation threatened to crush her beneath its weight. The night stretched on, the wind howled and the water dripped and Rebaa remained alone.

Alone.

Folding her arms over her knees, she dropped her head upon them and cried herself to sleep.

When she awoke, it was still dark. The wind outside had died and there was a breathlessness to the air. A chill crept along Rebaa's spine. Something had woken her. Something more than just a lull in the wind. Instinctively, she froze in place, staring hard at the empty mouth of the cave.

She could hear nothing in the silence, only the continued drip drip of the water behind her. But something was wrong. She knew it. Her skin was prickling, every instinct on alert.

She was being hunted.

Rebaa stopped breathing, waiting in the damp blackness. Had the monsters of the mountains picked up her trail? Terror thrilled through her at the thought. She bit her lip hard to keep from whimpering.

Then she felt it. A presence brushing against the edges of her wary senses. She concentrated harder and her heart skipped a beat in her chest. Not the monsters, but the approaching awareness bore the chilling focus of a ravening carnivore.

Crunch. Crunch. Crunch. The muffled sound of an approach in frozen snow outside told Rebaa it was already too late to run. The hunter was upon her. She flinched as a massive shadow fell across the mouth of the cave, blocking the paler blackness from outside. Blocking her escape. Rebaa felt it deliberate. An unseen nose sniffed the air as it searched for the potential meal it had been tracking. It knew she was here. It had followed her scent through the rocky wilderness.

Rebaa shrank back into her alcove as a triumphant snarl reached her ears. The heavy thud of paws and the skitter of stones across rocky ground announced the creature's entrance. It tested the air again and gave a hungry growl.

The presence was vast. Rebaa knew it instantly to be a bear. The thoughts were slow, deliberate and implacable. She was trapped. Her heart beat double time as panic thrilled to her fingertips. She fought to control her breathing and remain silent. The scent of her fear was already damning.

The snuffling drew closer. The bear's energy throbbed with excitement. It could certainly smell her but it couldn't see her. Yet. Rebaa gritted her teeth. She had to get out! But there was no way past. The passage was narrow. There was no way she would be fast enough. As soon as she moved so much as a finger, she would be lost.

Her baby kicked inside her, restless. Rebaa's thoughts sharpened instantly. It was not just her life hanging in the balance. She had to do something and fast. Concentrating hard on the rocks around her, she shifted her energy to match her surroundings. She slowed her heart rate, cooling her body. Hiding her presence was a skill that had always come easily to her. As a child she had driven her family to distraction. But that was when she had been strong. She was not strong now. She was hungry, traumatised and exhausted. She almost didn't have the power. Weak. Too weak.

The bear was so close now in the narrow passageway of the cave that she could feel its body heat. Rebaa held her breath, fighting to keep her concentration. The massive bulk swayed into view before her. Rebaa clenched her teeth and closed her eyes as the shaggy head swung around. Hot, damp breath saturated her face. The bear sniffed again. Rebaa tightened her fists, feeling the cold sweat in her palms. *Go away!* She thought at the creature. *There is nothing here!* But he did not move away. His powerful muzzle was inches from her face. He sniffed again. A confused rumble sounded in his chest.

This was no good. She could hide her presence all she liked. She could not hide her scent. The bear growled, sniffing harder. His lips peeled back from his thick teeth.

The illusion had failed. The only choice remaining was to run for her life. She needed a head start. Using what energy she had left, she touched the bear's thoughts. Rebaa gave him the overwhelming sense of another presence deeper inside the cave. The presence of the only thing that would distract the beast now. The threat of another bear.

The response was immediate. The bear's angry bellow reverberated though Rebaa's body. The great head swung away as the beast reared up to challenge its imagined adversary. Rebaa didn't waste her chance. Released from the bear's focus, she dropped her illusions and bolted. She had moments. The rocks cut at her feet through their wrappings as she fled. She hardly felt the pain. She had to get out!

The cave shuddered as the bear dropped back to the stones with a heavy thud. Confusion aggravated its thoughts. There was a pause before another furious bellow rent the air as it spotted its prey escaping from beneath its very nose.

Rebaa burst from the cave as the beast gave chase. Her eyes darted. Where could she go? Grindah's evil, silver eye was fully open in the sky, staring balefully down and revealing her clearly to her enemy. She scanned the ghostly landscape, searching for a bolt hole, anything to save herself. She tried to run faster, stumbling and falling and dragging herself back upright. She dared not look back. She didn't have to turn to know the bear was gaining on her with every mighty stride. The ground vibrated beneath her feet, signaling its deadly proximity.

Desperate, Rebaa reached again for the animal's mind. She tried to convince him she was not his prey. Within her forest home, even the most fearsome predators knew not to hunt the Achalaja. They lived in peace, mutual entities living together in harmonious balance. They were all part of the same Great Spirit that guided everything.

Rebaa was a long way from her forest home now. Her influence slipped from the bear's mind like water. The part of the Great Spirit inside, the part that guided him to hunt, to survive, was far too powerful. Rebaa's people could influence the Great Spirit but the Power of the Earth, once set, was beyond any of them. She could not sway this creature. She was as good as dead.

She felt the bear gathering itself to lunge before it even moved and dodged quickly. Heavy jaws snapped shut around empty air where her arm had just been. A tree rose up from the shadows before her and, acting on pure instinct, Rebaa scrambled into its branches. The feel of rough bark beneath her fingers was a distant relief.

Her people dwelt in trees, she was made for climbing, but her current condition made her cumbersome. With a snarl, the bear swiped upwards. Rebaa screamed as she felt the massive claws rake her right leg, ripping through the furs and deep into her skin. The pain was blinding. She almost lost her grip.

No, no, she chanted to herself, dragging herself higher even as she felt hot blood sliding down the torn skin of her calf.

She pushed herself to climb as high as she could go then clung there, staring down at her death. Blood and tears dripped down on to the bear's upturned face. Its beady eyes were furious, filled with frustration. Rebaa was only just out of reach. The tree was thin, a twig in comparison to the bear's monstrous strength. He could snap it like firewood if he so chose. She watched helplessly as the bear came to that same dreadful conclusion.

He reared up on his hind legs and began to batter the tree, hurling his weight against it again and again. The trunk creaked and splintered before the vicious onslaught.

Rebaa closed her eyes and cast one last prayer to Achala, asking for forgiveness as she prepared her soul to join with the Great One.

The spear came out of nowhere.

Chapter Three

Nen

Rebaa had barely finished her prayer to Achala when a challenging cry answered the angry snarls of the bear. She watched, feeling strangely disembodied as something streaked like lightening through the darkness and struck the bear full in the side, burying itself deep into the tough flesh. The creature threw back its head, jaws gaping wide as it roared its pain and surprise to the sky.

Staggering on its hind paws, it toppled over backwards. Rebaa watched in a kind of detached horror as the bear thrashed in the snow, turning everything dark red. A trickle of blood streamed from its mouth as the struggles became more and more feeble, then with a dying gurgle, the bear finally lay still.

For a few moments, Rebaa could not move. Her fingers were frozen in shock around the branches she had clung to for her very life. She stared down at the now lifeless form of her adversary. A violent trembling started all over her body and she knew it was not a good idea to remain in the branches. She could not afford to fall. As much as height offered protection, she would have to take her chances on the ground.

Stiffly and still feeling strangely outside of herself, Rebaa climbed back to the snow and rocks below. Her bleeding leg almost gave way beneath her. The injury was severe. If her situation had been precarious before, it was deadly now. The furs that covered her leg were soaked crimson. Her shaking grew worse. Falling to her knees, she vomited into the snow beside the great beast. Her stomach, already empty, dry heaved until her body ached.

When at last the retching stopped, she rolled on to her side and rested her hot cheek in the snow. It was nice. Listlessly, Rebaa stared at the fallen bear. She had seen so few of these creatures in her travels with Juran. It had been just her luck to have one stumble upon her while she slept. It shouldn't even have been active this deep into the winter Fury. He should have long ago disappeared into hibernation. She frowned, finding even that small motion an effort. Her large eyes scanned the shaggy body. She saw now that beneath the thick fur coat, the beast was emaciated. He had been in no condition for a long sleep. Despite herself, Rebaa's heart swelled with pity. The Furies were getting longer, colder, and it was not just Man that was suffering.

Her vision darkened. She blinked, fighting to keep focused. She really ought to move. She had to get up or she would perish in the snow. But she could not find it within herself to even raise an arm. Her eyes continued to rove over the bear's body and lighted on the object that must have killed it. A long, thick pole was protruding from its side.

The sight flashed a warning through Rebaa's fading consciousness. Such an object could only mean one thing. She had to get out of here. Struggling to get her boneless arms beneath her, Rebaa fought to rise.

"*Shalanaki?*" a throaty voice cut the air.

With a despairing moan, Rebaa sank back into the snow. It was too late. The owner of the spear had already arrived. It was not Achala's will that she should ever again live to see Her golden spirit rise above the horizon.

A pair of thickly booted feet stumped into view. They paused before Rebaa's face as her vision began to fade. The owner of the feet crouched down. Rebaa just had time to take in a broad face and a pair of black eyes staring at her impassively before the world turned black and she knew no more.

When Rebaa awoke, pain was all she knew. She hurt *everywhere*. Her muscles ached, her fingers and toes were searing. But the most prominent agony of all came from her right leg. Her wounds felt as if they were on fire! Instinctively, she tried to pull away, but a powerful grip closed around her leg and held her firm. Her eyes shot open.

She was inside a small, round cave. This one did not smell damp. It smelled of furs and burning wood. The walls glowed hot with the light of a fire. The pain in her leg intensified, accompanied by the sound of a sizzling hiss. Rebaa shrieked, eyes watering as she scrabbled at the stony ground with her fingers, fighting to escape. Helpless sobs escaped her raw throat. Somebody was burning her! The sickly sweet scent of scorched flesh filled her nostrils. Her empty stomach roiled dangerously and she retched in agony and disgust.

"*Runuk*," a throaty voice barked as the unseen grip tightened further. Rebaa began to cry openly in terror, fighting all the harder to get away from her captor. They were cooking her alive!

There was an impatient sigh before the grip on her searing leg loosened. Rebaa kicked backwards and heard a satisfying grunt as her foot contacted with what she guessed to be her captor's hand. She could feel a large presence behind her but she did not turn to take a look. She was loose! Boosted on adrenaline, Rebaa scrambled away towards the mouth of the cave. She might not get far but she sure as Achala was not going to give up without a fight! She tried to get her protesting legs under her to run.

"Stop."

Rebaa froze, shocked to hear a word she understood.

"Go. You die."

The words were not Achalaja but thickly accented versions of those used by the Cro clans. Rebaa rolled over slowly. At first her eyes were seared by the light of the small fire burning brightly in the center of the cave. Rebaa blinked. There was a large silhouette sitting alone before the flames. The figure was thickset and powerful in appearance. As her vision adjusted, she at first made out a mass of vividly orange hair that framed the head in a flaming halo. It flowed in a tangled mass down the thick shoulders. Next, the face came into focus. Milky-pale skin was stretched over coarse features and broad cheek bones. Black eyes glittered deeply from beneath a short but prominent brow. Despite the brutishness, the face was distinctly female. The stranger watched Rebaa carefully as she folded a pair of large, gnarled hands beneath the heavy, reddish-brown furs she wore.

Rebaa glanced down at her own grey-clad right leg. The furs were ripped away and the long claw marks that had slashed her smooth, red-gold skin were sealed with ugly, red and black burns. The pain of the searing still kept her teeth firmly clenched but she was no longer bleeding.

The shaggy head inclined towards the wounded limb. "Stop bad blood," was the halting explanation.

Rebaa remained hesitant, still unsure of this stranger's intent. She had been healed, in a fashion, which pointed to the fact that her captor must not intend to kill her. Not yet at least. The Achalaja woman reached out with her senses, probing the stranger's mind and relaxed very slightly. There was no ill intent, merely curiosity over-shadowed by a great sadness. Rebaa shied away from that sadness. It was like a dark chasm inside the stranger's soul.

Her eyes flickered over the pale, brutish face again. "You're a Thal?" she asked carefully.

The stranger frowned, struggling to grasp the words. She obviously knew a little of the Cro language but not much. Rebaa helped her by giving her a sense of the meaning straight into her mind.

The stranger blinked, her confusion clearing. "Yes. Thal. From-" she pointed upwards.

Unthinkingly, Rebaa followed her direction, frowning up at the stone ceiling until the Thal's actual meaning dawned on her.

"The north?" Rebaa guessed. From her knowledge of Thals, they could survive in the harshest of lands inside the northern wastes where no other people could remain, hunting the giant tusked beasts of the ice. Rebaa eyed the shaggy, long-haired furs of her unexpected companion. They bore no resemblance to the comparatively short-haired, grey wolf furs that she wore. She had never seen such garments. "You're a long way from home," Rebaa commented, cocking her head as she conveyed her message both verbally and mentally.

The Thal woman shrugged. "Cold times get worse. People move south or die."

Rebaa shuddered, knowing the truth of that. "Where are your people?"

The deep set eyes grew shadowed. "No, no. Lost."

"You're alone?"

The shaggy head nodded sadly. "Like you."

Rebaa found herself unable to meet that infinitely sad and somehow all too knowing gaze. "Yes."

The silence stretched as each of them sank into their own separate thoughts.

"Come," the Thal woman broke the awkward silence first, beckoning. "Fire. Warm."

The dark gaze was now inviting, hopeful. The Thal gestured to the ground beside her next to the glowing beast. Rebaa hesitated again. It was true she could sense no malice from the stranger but still...

"*Shalanaki,*" her companion held up her rough and empty hands. "You freezing in snow. Need warm."

She wasn't wrong. Rebaa could not feel her hands or her feet even inside their thick wrappings. The cold was definitely getting worse. The promise of warmth overpowered her reservations and Rebaa began to move warily back to the fireside. She hissed as the skin on her burned leg pulled and seared. Eyes watering, she twisted and clutched at her calf in agony.

Clucking her tongue sympathetically, the Thal woman got up, her every motion was slow and measured. Rebaa guessed she was trying not to startle her with any sudden movements. Striding to the cave entrance, the stranger reached outside and returned with a great handful of snow. Keeping her eyes upon Rebaa's to convey she meant no harm, she dumped the icy handful straight on to Rebaa's tortured flesh. Rebaa gasped in shock, then her breath rushed out in a great sigh of relief as her pain eased, numbed by the treatment.

"Thank you," she whispered in helpless gratitude. The Thal took her elbow and Rebaa could no longer find it in herself to resist as she was gently guided to the fire. Thick furs were spread out all around it and the stranger laid her upon them before moving back to the other side of the flames, allowing Rebaa the comfort of space. Rebaa groaned, her tense body melting in relief as the heat washed over her. Her fingers and toes once again seared as one extreme met another. She endured it with a fierce pleasure.

There had been a time when fire had frightened her. It was a skill her own people did not possess. Out in these cold wastes, however, it was a blessing, a life giver. She stretched out her hands, only wanting to be nearer.

"Hungry?"

Fear subsiding, Rebaa quite suddenly became aware of the smell of cooking meat and spied the hunk of browned flesh spitted over the fire. Despite her lasting aversion to meat, her mouth watered as her forgotten stomach growled. Her baby kicked. He was hungry. She soothed him with a thought. He was becoming more aware, his thoughts and feelings hazing against her own. It was nearly time for him to greet the world. She would need all her strength for that fast approaching ordeal. She looked across the flames with pleading eyes.

The Thal woman understood. She pulled the sizzling meat from the fire. Using pieces of worn leather hide, she took hold of it and tore it in two, handing one half of the bounty to Rebaa. Rebaa did not wait for it to cool. She immediately sank her teeth into the scorched flesh, not caring when it burned her mouth. Her protesting stomach eased with the first scalding swallow.

Her companion gave a throaty laugh, coarse features alight with amusement. "He tried to eat you, now you eat him!"

Rebaa had nearly finished her helping but almost brought it back up as the meaning of the Thal's words hit home. She was eating the bear! Juran had always known better than to draw attention to what went into her stomach. "Please, don't," she warned, nauseous.

Rebaa was surprised to see the stranger's expression become apologetic. "You Dryad? Wood sprite?"

Rebaa frowned. She had heard her people called many names on her journey. These were new.

"Achalaja," she corrected.

"Acha- Achaja-" her companion gave up. "Hard. You Dryads live in woods. Down." She pointed.

"South? Yes."

"Eat plants," she pointed at herself and then her ear. *I hear*, Rebaa read the meaning, "talk animals?"

Rebaa nodded warily. "In a way."

"How?" The Thal's face was eager. She was hungry, desperate even, for conversation.

Rebaa sighed. This was going to be difficult. "When the blessed Achala came from the skies to create our people, she made us with the essence of the Great Spirit and gifted us with an awareness of him."

"Great Spirit?"

"The very life force of the earth, every plant, every creature, a great and powerful energy that guides all life. Achala's Gift means that my people can influence and use the energy. We are a part of the Great Spirit. I can hear him in the wind, in the water, in the murmurings of the animals. They are his children, the vassals of his wisdom, and it is they who preserve his balance. My people were tasked by Achala Herself to learn from them all."

Rebaa realised she had got rather carried away and wasn't sure how much her companion had followed. She marvelled at the strangeness of her situation, telling of her people's origins while sitting in a cave with a creature whom those very same people would consider an unnatural abomination.

"Why not talk bear? Tell not hunt?"

"I tried," Rebaa rubbed her face tiredly. "Sometimes the will of the Great One is just too powerful."

The Thal frowned but accepted slowly. Rebaa was sure she did not fully understand. It mattered little. She was beyond exhaustion. Too tired to explain Seeing to someone who was Blind. Rebaa felt her eyelids beginning to droop. She fought against them. She still did not know how safe she was here.

"You wear clothes of Cro not Dryad. They catch you? How escape?"

Rebaa grimaced. She was in no state of mind to relive her ordeal and certainly not with a stranger. "It's a long story." Her heavy eyes closed traitorously against her efforts. Her stomach was full and she was so warm…

"Baby." The Thal patted her own belly. "Soon."

The words ripped the exhaustion aside. Instantly alert, Rebaa struggled to keep her face impassive even as her heart thudded. If this Thal guessed her baby's heritage then she was as good as dead. "Yes," she hedged. She hoped her companion would simply assume the father was Achalaja and not pry further.

"Should not be alone."

No, she should not. Rebaa pressed her lips together to suppress her longing for the one she would never see again. Her anger burned anew. It was all his fault! He should have fled. They should have taken their chances. A tear slipped down her cheek. She brushed it away angrily. He had made his choice. He had abandoned her. She pushed her grief down deep. If she faced it, she would not be able to function and she needed all of her wits.

"Not alone now," the Thal woman comforted. "I watch you tonight. You safe now."

Rebaa sighed, her defences crumbling before the open gaze. The Thal's energy was strangely comforting, motherly, even. She felt the aching weariness wash over her anew. "Why are you helping me?" she gathered the will to ask.

"I alone, too," came the melancholy reply. "Long time."

Despite everything, Rebaa's heart went out to the lonely creature opposite her. She stared empathetically into the black eyes peering across the flickering flames. She could sense nothing more than a heartfelt sincerity and a deep, desperate desire for companionship, however brief. Rebaa made up her mind. She lay down upon the thick furs lining the fire, accepting the offered comforts. She would trust her new companion. For now.

"What's your name?" Rebaa asked as she slid towards unconsciousness.

"Nen."

Rebaa smiled. "Rebaa."

Chapter Four

Need

Rebaa woke to the thick scent of smoke curling from the dying fire. She had slept fitfully, her dreams filled with monsters and death. She remembered waking often with a cry on her lips, clutching her chest against the raw, aching loss. Each time she had found the Thal woman sitting close by, watching her with that sad, knowing expression. She had been singing. The songs she sang were strange to Rebaa but had possessed a soothing power that had returned her to sleep each time, wrapping her in a cocoon of comfort.

Rebaa sat up. Light was streaming in through the cave entrance. Achala had already risen. Against all odds, Rebaa had lived to see Her golden spirit again after all. The thought gave her renewed hope.

Rebaa glanced around. She was alone. Her new companion was nowhere to be seen. Cautiously, she got to her feet and studied her surroundings. The cave walls were cold and grey now the fire had burned low but the space had the feel of having been lived in for a long time. The ground had been cleared of loose rocks, all of which were piled neatly against the walls. Furs were strewn around. A couple of spears were leaning near the entrance. They were a less refined weapon than those Rebaa had become accustomed to seeing, yet still deadly in appearance. She did not study them for long. Her attention was drawn back to the curving walls where dozens of reliefs had been scratched into the grey stone.

Limping heavily on her wounded leg, Rebaa moved to take a closer look. There were many pictures of animals, of birds, bears, lions, horses. They were crudely drawn but still very distinct. There were yet more creatures that she did not even recognise. Giant beasts with great curving tusks sprouting from under a long snake-like limb, located where most ordinary animals' noses would be. How odd. The most numerous of the creations, however, were the images of people. Rebaa ran her fingers over the rocks, feeling the nuances beneath her skin.

It seemed that each picture was telling its own story. Here was a scratching of a settlement. All the people appeared happy and at peace. There, Rebaa could make out a hunting scene. The people had brought down one of the tusked beasts. She moved along the wall, trailing her fingertips, fascinated. Some of the images were not so happy. One clearly showed a battle between peoples. Many were dead. Rebaa shuddered away from that image. The memories it conjured were far too fresh and horrific for her to face. She didn't need any more nightmares. She moved swiftly on.

The next picture showed a woman holding a baby. Rebaa lingered over that one, her hands unconsciously moving to her belly where her own baby dozed beneath her heart. Somehow the image was sad. Rebaa turned around and saw another picture where a figure appeared to be fleeing from others who were hurling stones. She only caught a glimpse, however, before a deep, throaty voice called from behind her.

"Wake?"

Rebaa flinched and spun to face the cave entrance. Nen had appeared and was watching her carefully. Her large hands were covered in red gore. Rebaa shuddered but nodded in answer.

"Come, help," Nen beckoned with her bloody fingers. The Thal turned and disappeared back into the white landscape beyond. Rebaa hesitated for a moment then followed. Her leg hurt, the skin over the burns was stiff and pulled with every motion. She gritted her teeth. She would get some more snow on it.

As she stepped out of the dim cave, the gleaming light bouncing off the endless white was blinding. The cold, fresh air was sharp in her nostrils. Rebaa blinked rapidly until her eyes adjusted. She could see they were not far up the shoulder of the mountain, the cave was set into a sloping hill covered in dead grass and tumbled rocks. The landscape fell away into the vast plain below.

A movement to the right caught her attention. Nen was walking away down the slope, steady and surefooted. Rebaa started after her but quickly found it wasn't as easy as the Thal woman made it look. The rocks were treacherous underfoot and progress was slow. Rebaa tested every step. When she finally reached their destination, she took one look and had to brace herself against a wave of nausea.

Nen was standing beside the grisly body of the massive cave bear. She had quite obviously skinned it and carved great chunks of meat from its bones. The scent of blood and raw flesh overpowered all else. With a sharpened flint knife, Nen began carving out another huge hunk of flesh. She glanced up at Rebaa in grim satisfaction.

"Good kill," she indicated the stacks of meat cuts and the massive, thick hide piled behind her. "Plenty food. Not hunt again for long."

Rebaa forced a smile, trying her best to appear pleased when all she really wanted to do was turn away. Such things were still not natural to her. *Survival, survival,* she chanted to herself. That was all that mattered. She pressed her lips together to hold back the sadness and regret. She wondered just how Achalaja she really was anymore. She had violated too many things that were sacred to her people in the name of survival. She hoped Achala could forgive her and understand. The baby kicked. A tear escaped her eye. There were some things she was certain would never be forgiven or understood.

Nen began to heft the heavy pelt she had taken from the dead bear.

"Help?" she asked again.

With a shudder, Rebaa moved down to help drag the hideous thing back up the hill to the cave. It was still dripping with sinew and fat and was a dead weight, slimy beneath her fingers. It smelled awful. Of sickly sweet death. Rebaa almost couldn't bring herself to touch it. The only thought that kept her there was the need to repay Nen for feeding her and providing her with a night of warmth and safety.

Even so, she did not feel she was of that much help as they tugged and heaved the bloody hide over the rocks. Nen was a full head and shoulders taller than Rebaa was and massively strong. This comparison wasn't unusual. Most beings were bigger and stronger than the Achalaja.

Rebaa was panting hard and holding her side when they finally reached the mouth of the cave. She collapsed to the hard floor, her legs refusing to hold her any longer. Her wounds burned. She reached outside and doused them with another handful of snow. For the first time, she felt like removing her thick coverings to cool down.

Nen's face was filled with open amusement. "Dryad not strong."

Rebaa chuckled. "I guess Dryads don't need to be, Nen." She tapped her temple. "We have different means."

Nen frowned then. "Not good for you." She patted her stomach. "Rest. I carry." She stooped to pick up a smooth stone that fitted comfortably into her large hand. One curving edge had been knapped into a sharp blade. "You strip." Nen pointed to the fur.

Rebaa wrinkled her nose. She knew what Nen was asking. She wanted her to prepare and clean the skin. She clenched her teeth together and braced herself for an unpleasant morning.

By the time Nen had finished bringing the rest of the bear meat up the hill, Rebaa was covered to the elbows in greasy fat, stray hair and stinking bits of flesh. The pelt was finally clean and ready for further preparation, however.

Nen could see the open disgust on her face. A smile touched her wide lips. She was shoving most of the meat supply into a snow bank outside to keep it fresh. The hunks had also been stripped of what little fat had been on the bear, keeping only the lean meat, further lengthening its life. Once she had finished her task, Nen picked up the cleaned bear-skin and beckoned to Rebaa with one gnarled hand. Her lips were still twitching with suppressed mirth at Rebaa's disgruntled expression as she walked back out into the snow without a word.

Rebaa guessed she was supposed to follow. Keeping her stinking arms as far away from her furs as possible, she limped after her companion, wondering what other unpleasantness could possibly lie in wait.

Nen had set out in the opposite direction from the bear, slinging its skin across her broad shoulders as she trudged through the snow. The pelt was much lighter now it had been stripped of its wet, excess flesh and Nen easily managed the load on her own.

Following along, Rebaa glanced into the crisp blue sky above. The spirit of Achala was now at her zenith. Not that Rebaa would know that from the bitterness of the air. Achala's golden face shone down but Her touch held little warmth. Rebaa frowned worriedly. Achala's power of late had waned, letting her evil brother's cold times increase.

Before her journey had begun, Rebaa's people had started to whisper, whisper that Grindah was finally winning the battle for dominance in the heavens. Rebaa shuddered. From the beginning of time, her forefathers had passed down the teaching that if Grindah ever grew more powerful than his sister, it would signal the end of the world. The end of the Achalaja and their way of life.

Feeling the weakness of Achala's light now, Rebaa hoped her ancestors' teachings were wrong. It wouldn't have been the first thing her people had been wrong about. She tried to ignore the plume of her breath freezing on the midday air. She had enough to worry about.

The sound of running water pulled her from her melancholy. Nen had stopped and was pointing ahead over the top of an outcropping of rocks. The sound was coming from there. Rebaa joined her companion and looked down. A sparkling mountain stream was rushing before her on its way down to the plain below. Nen motioned to her, mimicking washing her arms.

"Ah," Rebaa said, understanding. "Thank you." She picked her way over the icy rocks to the fast flowing water. She shuddered to think how cold it would be but anything was better than putting up with the mess she was in right now. She sank to her knees and dipped her arms into the flow. She almost cried out at the shock of it. It was freezing! She washed as quickly as she could, scrubbing away the greasy fat and hairs sticking nauseatingly to her skin. She was shivering violently when she had finished.

Nen caught hold of her and rubbed her arms quickly. Rebaa was surprised by the physical contact but found she could not protest. Nen's hands were rough but pleasantly warm.

Now that Rebaa was clean, they turned their attention to the skin. It needed to be preserved before it started to fester. Nen soaked the hide in the running water, then pulled it out and between them they rung it dry. This process was repeated again and again. The day was growing dark when Nen was finally satisfied.

As Achala set, Rebaa let Nen lead her back to the cave. Her very bones ached with exhaustion from the day's work. The lack of sleep wasn't helping. Once they were back inside, she sank wearily onto the furs by the fire and watched distantly as her Thal companion spread the half prepared skin flat on the cold ground before turning to build the flames back up.

Tired as she felt, Rebaa knew she must force her mind to sort through her situation. This little interlude had been a blessing she had not foreseen but she must be moving on. She still had a long way to go.

"What think?" Nen asked.

Rebaa opened her half closed eyes. Her concern must have shown on her face. "I'm thinking about how I'm going to get back to my people."

A flicker of sadness and disappointment touched Nen's face. "You should not be alone," she admonished. "Stay here until cold time over. After baby born. Then find people."

Rebaa shifted uncomfortably. The generous offer was tempting and she wished she could take it and spend the Fury inside this cosy cave. She liked this Thal woman. Nen had a good spirit. The pending birth, however, made such an agreement impossible. Nen could not see her baby. She would need to be long gone before then.

"I'm sorry, Nen," she said, regretfully. "I must leave. I have to get back."

"Father waiting?" Nen guessed.

No, Rebaa thought, *father dead.* Instead, she nodded, glad that Nen had jumped to that mistaken conclusion. "Yes, father waiting," she lied. "I must get back to him."

Nen accepted her words sadly. "Stay just bit longer? Until recover? Still tire easily and leg hurt." Her eyes were hopeful, needful even. The longing in them tugged at Rebaa's heart.

She plucked at the soft fur upon which she sat. She supposed Nen was right, although her leg was probably stronger now than Nen could guess. All Achalaja could heal themselves to a degree, although some were more skilled than others. Throughout the day, Rebaa had been directing what little energy she had to spare at her wounds, encouraging the flesh to knit and become whole. But it wasn't much and it was still far from healed. She needed to regain more strength otherwise she would not get very far.

That was what she told herself. Deep down, she knew she was simply clutching at any excuse to put off the impossible danger she faced for a short while more. Could she blame herself?

"That would be nice," she admitted finally with a soft smile, then frowned. Nen seemed so desperate for company. Why was such a caring being living in isolation? "Why are you not with your own people, Nen?" she asked curiously. "Why are you alone?"

Rebaa watched as the glittering light in the deep-set eyes grew dim. The ordinarily open soul closed with a snap. "Not talk." Nen shook her large head evasively.

Rebaa guessed her meaning from the reluctance she could feel in the Thal woman's heart. "You don't want to talk about it?"

Nen shook her head again, avoiding Rebaa's gaze. Tears were beginning to form in the gentle eyes.

Swamped by guilt, Rebaa got up and went to her. She couldn't help it. She brushed away the tears, wanting to offer what comfort she could. She wasn't the only one battling painful memories, it seemed.

Nen leaned against her gratefully and, with a sigh, Rebaa made her decision. She could not fix whatever Nen had suffered anymore than she could fix her own past but she would do one thing for this woman who had saved her life.

"Don't worry, Nen. I will stay for a little while longer." She smiled. "I cannot refuse the offer of a friend."

Nen's eyes lit up, burning brightly with fervent hope, her pain forgotten. "Friend?"

Rebaa smiled sadly back at her. "Yes, Nen. Friend."

Chapter Five

Stories

"No!" Rebaa sat bolt upright beneath her warm covers, the cry of denial fresh on her lips. The horrors of her nightmare evaporated into the darkness of the cave. She panted, clutching her chest as her heart tried to beat its way out of it. Hugging the furs to her, she tried to stop the shaking, feeling cold despite the glowing of the fire.

She looked around quickly for her companion but Nen was nowhere to be seen. She was alone. At first she was alarmed but then the sound of a voice softly singing floated to her from just outside the cave mouth. Rebaa relaxed.

Keeping the fur blanket wrapped firmly around her shoulders, she got up and crept out into the night. Nen was sitting on a jumble of rocks, her face upturned towards the dark sky as she sang. Still haunted by the horrors of her nightmare, Rebaa sat close beside her friend, taking comfort from her steady presence. Nen stopped her song.

"Dream bad?" she asked in a hushed voice, her deep eyes shadowed in the darkness.

"Yes." Rebaa shivered. It was so cold out here beyond the warmth of the cave. The smell of frost was strong on the crisp air. Her breath rose in white plumes. Rebaa did not realise she had been crying until Nen reached out to brush away the tears freezing upon her face.

"Talk?" Nen offered.

Rebaa shook her head in one quick motion. She did not want to speak about it. She would never be able to put words to the horror she had witnessed or the loss she had experienced. If she tried to speak, the thin walls she had built around her emotions would crumble. She had to keep them at bay.

"*Shalanaki,*" Nen murmured.

Rebaa cocked her head. "What does *shalanaki* mean?" she asked.

Nen shrugged her shoulders. "Thal use as greeting and parting. Means close like 'peace'."

Rebaa smiled. "That's nice." The night was so silent it began to press in on her. She wanted to ask more questions to keep Nen talking. Her friend's voice kept the memories in check. "What were you singing about?"

Nen blinked. "I sing praise to Eron. Ask him to forgive and watch over."

"Eron?"

"Great being," said Nen. "Came down from sky with brothers and sisters and made the Thal people." She tilted her face towards the blackness with its many burning spirits. She waved her hand against the endless purplish line that glowed through the middle. "Came here following sacred sky path. Gave people life."

Rebaa was silent for a moment as she stared up into the vastness above. "Your Eron is like Achala. Our most holy came from the skies at the beginning of time to create the Achalaja people and teach us how to be one with the Great Spirit and his Children."

Nen's face was filled with wonder. "Maybe Achala one of Eron sisters from the sky?"

Rebaa smiled. "Maybe. Does Eron guide your people still?" she asked.

Nen shook her head. "Left us. Our spirit men say Eron took to sky when we fail his teaching and went to live alone in forbidden mountain. We not see him. Do not know where to find. He ignore us. We anger him. Achala still with you?"

Rebaa folded her arms against her chest. "No, she had to leave us, too. Our teachings say that her brother, Grindah, grew jealous of my people and sought to destroy us out of spite. Achala fought him and was forced to leave us lest their battle destroy the world. She dragged her brother with her and imprisoned him in the sky. She remains there also, guarding against his return as she watches over us, continuing to give us life. She is the great Golden Mother of the Day Sky." Rebaa shuddered and pointed to the silver eye staring balefully from the far horizon. "The night is Grindah's, his spirit trapped forever in that great eye. He watches us in the darkness of the night, ready to expose the unwary. He and Achala are doomed to chase each other through the heavens until the end of time, holding each other in balance. Heat and cold. Day and night. It is said if Achala ever falters, if she ever falls to her brother, the Furies that come will last many lifetimes and our people will cease to be. Only Achala's power protects our way of life and keeps us safe from our enemies." Watching the bitter landscape rolling out before her, the fear of the day crept back into Rebaa's heart. "I am afraid, Nen. Afraid that that time is already upon us. The Furies grow longer and our enemies, the children of Grindah, grow bolder. My people are weakening. Our forests are dying." She stared helplessly up at the sky. "Maybe our time has come."

Nen reached out and took her small hand. "My people grow weak, too. Cro get stronger. Eron not protect us. I sing for his return along the sky path. Save people." She smiled sadly. "He not answer yet. Maybe our time come, too."

Grimly, Rebaa returned her grip and for a while they both stared up into the endless night, Thal and Achalaja together. It was easy to imagine they were the last of their kind sitting there alone in the vastness. Nothing more than dust motes caught up in some vast plan. The world was changing and Rebaa wondered if her people were even meant to be a part of it. It was a saddening thought.

"Sleep?" Nen offered at last, bringing Rebaa back to earth. "I watch. You need rest."

Rebaa gripped her hand. "No," she whispered. "I don't want to go back to sleep. I'll watch tonight and keep the fire going."

Nen's eyes searched hers for a brief moment then nodded her consent. She rose and went back inside the cave, settling down on the furs next to the fire. Rebaa remained outside for a little while longer but could not stand the loneliness for long. She felt in danger of floating away, like the dust mote she was, and becoming lost in the vastness above, to be swallowed up and forgotten. Grindah's eye stared on unforgivingly.

Rebaa moved quickly back into the embrace of the cave. This solid, immovable rock shelter was a far cry from the living, ever whispering canopies that had protected her through childhood, but at least it blocked out the unnatural, terrifying openness. She added more fuel to the fire and sat down beside Nen, wrapping the covers more tightly around her slight shoulders. She stared into the flames, letting the warmth and light banish the gnawing fears of the dark. Reaching out, she took hold of Nen's hand once more. It remained firmly in hers all through the long night.

Chapter Six

Threat

The next day dawned with the promise of snow in the air. During the night, the clouds had rolled over and the skies were now a flat, endless grey, stretching from one horizon to the other. Achala's sacred face was entirely masked.

"Lot of snow coming." Nen commented, as she reached out of the cave to bring in more meat to thaw by the fire for later.

Rebaa's heart sank. This was bad news. She could not afford to be trapped here before the baby was born. Nen's easy acceptance would end as soon as she saw what it was that she bore. But if she went back on her promise to Nen and left the shelter of the cave now, she would get caught in the coming blizzards and she would surely die. She was caught between two impossibilities. She stared up at the ominously silent skies. Achala was indeed punishing her for her forbidden heresy.

Nen, however, was busy scrutinising Rebaa's clothes. "Not enough," she spoke. "You journey. Need better." She moved over to the giant bear skin that was ready for tanning. "Bear skin good. Great tough. Warm. Better chance."

It seemed that Nen had made up her mind to spend Rebaa's remaining time here preparing her fully for the journey ahead, making sure she had the best chance of survival. Rebaa's heart swelled with gratitude. She wished she could do more for her new found friend than offer a few scant days of companionship.

"Why are you being so good to me?" she asked, half to herself.

Nen frowned. "Want to make sure you find people. You baby survive. Most important thing."

Rebaa grew very conscious of the heavy swell of her belly beneath her wolf furs. Yes, he had to survive. It was important. More important than anything else. Somehow, that knowledge transcended even her own maternal instincts. She had to make sure this baby survived. She smiled at Nen. "You are a blessing from Achala herself. Maybe she isn't abandoning me after all."

Nen blushed as she handed Rebaa crushed bits of bark and leaves. They rubbed these into the dried skin until it was deeply stained with the essence of the trees.

"Tell me about your people, Nen," she asked to distract herself from her worries. "You seem to know a little of mine but I know nothing of yours."

Nen raised an eyebrow. "No?"

"No, my people do not take much interest in anything beyond our forests."

Nen was silent for a long while. Rebaa guessed she was gathering her mastery of the words. She wondered distantly how Nen had come to know part of the Cro tongue. She got the impression Nen knew quite a lot of the world.

Nen handed her the tools needed and instructed her on what was necessary to make new garments. The snow started to fall outside and the world took on that peculiar silence that came with the blanketing. Nen used a sharp flint knife to cut up the bear pelt into the needed sizes. Rebaa tried not to wrinkle her nose when the Thal woman started chewing on the edges of one piece, softening it up in preparation for stitching.

"People live where Eron lead us long ago." Nen said finally, softly spitting bits of stray hair from her tongue. "Vast places further up. Dangerous. Life hard. We live in caves like this or in bone and skin shelters. Eron showed us how to make flame, how to make tools. Hunt the Great Ones."

"Great ones?"

Nen pointed to her etchings on the cave walls. Rebaa followed her gesture and saw again the image of a massive tusked beast with a snake for a nose.

"Mighty spirits," Nen murmured. "If young man kill one, greatly revered by people. He become worthy warrior. May choose any woman he want."

"I see," Rebaa murmured.

A sadness fell over Nen's face. "My Alok killed Great One. He was going to choose me. Make strong children."

Rebaa was quick to catch the shift in Nen's hitherto easy energy. She was in pain. Rebaa felt it keenly. The great sadness that she had felt when they first met yawned open like a bottomless chasm. "What happened?"

Nen opened her mouth to respond but was cut off when a sharp howl from outside split the muffled air. Rebaa jumped. Nen's head snapped around towards the cave mouth. Her eyes sparked with a sudden mix of fury and fear as she scrambled to her feet. She grabbed one of her spears from the cave wall. The other she threw to Rebaa. "Weapon. Need." She instructed. Her voice was tight.

"What's wrong?" Rebaa asked, made uneasy by her friend's reaction.

"Men." Nen replied tersely. "Not animal." She crept out of their shelter, hand firmly on her spear.

"Nen!" Rebaa whispered, alarmed. "Don't go out."

"Just look. No see me. Make sure leave. You stay." Oddly, beside her friend's fear, Rebaa thought she could detect a faint sense of longing, of a desperate hope. Before she could be certain, however, Nen had disappeared into the falling snow.

Rebaa hissed in frustration. She waited, tense and alert but, as the moments crept by, the solitude and the silence began to crawl over her skin. Her imagination ran away with her, conjuring the worst. What if one of the strangers got around Nen and caught her here alone? The thought had her instantly on her feet. She picked up the spear Nen had thrown in her direction. Her fingers didn't even meet around the pole. It was twice as tall as she was but she clutched it to her nonetheless, flinching at every little noise. The silence stretched. Why had Nen gone out? Her terror had been obvious. Why risk getting caught?

In the end, Rebaa could bear it no longer. Nen had told her to stay but she would not wait around to be trapped. She did not want to be alone. Cautiously, she crept to the cave entrance and looked around. All she could see was white land, grey sky and the falling snow in between. She glanced at the ground and saw Nen's tracks leading off towards the bear kill. She cast her higher awareness in that direction. A herd of oxen was picking its way through the rocks somewhere further up the slope, their huge individual energies burned hot in Rebaa's mind as they searched for better grazing. Further down, Nen was not far away. Rebaa sighed in relief. Beyond her, Rebaa could now sense the strangers. There were about ten of them, she guessed. Silently, she stole out after Nen. She was terrified that her friend may be seen and captured… or worse.

The Thal woman was crouched stealthily behind an outcropping of rocks when Rebaa caught up with her. The snow had fallen on her reddish furs, blending her into the landscape. Rebaa crouched beside her. Nen glanced at her in irritation then turned back to stare further down the slope. Her black eyes raked over the scene with a strange kind of hunger. Again, Rebaa felt that faint taste of hope, though it was slowly fading. Baffled, she followed her friend's gaze.

Standing in a scattered formation around the bear kill, was a group of Cro. She instantly recognised their tall forms, long legs and lean bodies made for running. Their furs were well made, better fitted than Nen's crude coverings. Their eyes glittered with a fierce intelligence, minds quick, agile and adaptable.

Nen hissed angrily. "Evil men." She spat. "Takers and killers!"

Rebaa barely heard her. She was watching the Cro below with growing trepidation. These men were dangerous. They were picking over the kill, studying the area. Rebaa knew what they were thinking. The bear had been stripped of its skin and meat but it was obvious that the work had not been carried out by tooth and claw. They were examining the ground, assessing the strength of the other people who must have made the kill.

"Nen, we have to go," Rebaa whispered on an urgent breath. "They'll wonder who took all that meat. They can see our tracks. Only two tracks. They outnumber us."

Nen growled, gripping her spear as if she would very much like to plant it between the shoulder blades of one of the Cro.

"Come on!" Rebaa urged. "We need to hide our footprints!" She began to creep away pulling Nen behind her. She grabbed a loose branch from the base of one of the bare trees and started sweeping the snow behind them. She hoped it would be enough.

Unfortunately, she had been concentrating so hard on smothering their tracks, she had not paid enough attention to the ground beneath her feet as she edged backwards. A loose rock dislodged beneath her foot and with a soft cry, she tumbled onto her backside. The rock skittered away, bouncing loudly down the slope, echoing all around the surrounding foothills.

Nen and Rebaa froze, not daring to breathe.

There was a moment of absolute silence before shouts from below broke the stillness, followed by the tread of muffled feet running in their direction. Rebaa shared one terrified glance with Nen. Without a word, they threw caution to the wind and ran for their lives.

It was a futile effort. As with the bear before, Rebaa could feel their quarry rapidly gaining on them. The Cro were made for running. The best hunters. Nen was built for tireless strength. Rebaa for climbing. She was also still nursing a serious injury. This was not a race they could win.

Howls of triumph sounded behind as their pursuers caught sight of them fleeing ahead. Rebaa gasped, hobbling now, and tried to run faster. She was almost spent when Nen grabbed her and yanked her back into the shelter of their cave.

Doubled over, Rebaa fought to catch her breath. She clutched at a pain in her side. It was hopeless. This cave was no protection. It was a trap with no way out. A new fear took hold in Rebaa's heart. Juran's clan had conquered many of the Cro territories in the area. If this was one of those displaced tribes and one of them happened to recognise her... Rebaa stifled a cry and held on tightly to her spear.

Nen stood defiant in the mouth of the cave as the baying of their pursuers grew steadily louder. She was deathly pale but her eyes were fierce. "They not take me," she swore. Stooping, she grabbed a rock from one of her neat piles against the cave walls. Rebaa latched on to her determination, letting it give her strength. They would not go down without a fight. She grabbed her own rock and stood firmly beside her companion.

Even so, her heart quailed as the dark figures materialised out of the snow. They drew to a halt and paced restlessly at a distance of about fifty paces. They stared up the slope at the two women standing waiting for them in the cave mouth, hesitant and unsure. They had no way to tell for certain that Nen and Rebaa were alone. The cave could conceal a larger tribe. The Cro group was not strong in number and they were not stupid.

It would not take them long to figure out the truth, however, and they would move to either capture or kill the threat in this new found territory. Rebaa locked her teeth together to stop them chattering. Did this particular tribe capture foreign women to keep and use? Whatever their preference, kill or capture, nothing was to stop them from having some fun first.

The standoff broke as the lead figure started up the hill towards the cave. With a fierce cry, Nen hurled her heavy rock. The approaching man dodged at the last moment and the stone flew through the space where his head had been. Had it made contact, it would have killed him outright.

A fierce grin broke over the Cro's face. His eyes glittered with an unpleasant promise. He ripped his clothing apart, exposing the whole of his powerful and masculine body, displaying his large manhood in a show of primal dominance and threat. He raised his spear in the air and roared his challenge. He charged, bringing the rest of his men with him.

Shrieking her defiance, Nen hurled rock after rock at the approaching Cro. Some of her missiles found their targets. A few of the men crumpled to the ground, bones shattered by the force of the impacts. The others did not slow their charge, driven as they were by a raging passion and blood lust. Rebaa hurled a few of her own stones but they fell pathetically short and rolled harmlessly past their enemies. Still they charged. She and Nen were lost.

In that blackest moment of despair, a memory tugged at Rebaa's mind, fighting for her attention. She paused, thinking quickly. The solution struck like a bolt of lightening. It was their only chance! She had to make it work.

Gathering her strength, she reached out to the energies further up the hill. They were still there. The oxen. It was a fairly large herd. Rebaa needed only to get them to run. Gathering her will, she planted the sense of threat into their wary minds. A large cave lion was stalking the herd from above. She threw all of her concentration into that one image.

There was a second of awful silence. Then the ground began to tremble beneath their feet. Rebaa let out a crow of triumph. She had done it! Feeling the ominous vibration, their enemies paused in their charge, uncertainty flickering in their eyes.

Nen turned to her with the same anxious expression. "Rebaa?"

Rebaa did not waste time explaining. She had eyes only for her enemies, glaring down at them in fierce triumph as the herd of massive herbivores came crashing down the hillside, breaking all around the cave in an unstoppable force.

Watching death bear down upon them, the Cro dropped their weapons and fled for their lives. But even they could not outrun the stampeding oxen. They were charged into the ground and trampled beneath the crushing hooves. Only one escaped. Rebaa saw him fleeing into the distance. He did not look back and soon was swallowed up by the landscape. She felt a prickle of apprehension as she stared after him but there was nothing she could do about him now.

The danger was past. Exhausted, Rebaa sank down to her knees. Manipulating the oxen had drained her.

The silence that followed was loaded. Nen seemed unable to take in the swift turn of events. She stared after their enemies, eyes darting, one raised fist still clutching a rock in a white-knuckled grip.

"Relax, Nen," Rebaa soothed in a weary voice. "They're gone now. Dead."

Nen turned her head sharply, eyes wild. Her raised fist trembled. Rebaa moved over to their dying fire. She added a few more logs and poked it with a stick to breathe new life into it. She tried to busy herself with the mundane to distract her own self from their brush with death. Her hands shook.

Nen began to pace up and down, radiating nervous energy.

"I'm glad my brother taught me that trick when we were children," Rebaa said softly, attempting to sound strong.

Nen stopped pacing to face her. She still appeared a little wild. Rebaa kept talking in a soothing voice.

"Barias and I were playing where we shouldn't," Rebaa retold, getting lost in the memory. "We had ventured to the edge of our forest, which was dangerous. We almost got caught by the Elders who had come to look for us. There was a deer herd browsing nearby. Barias made them think they were being chased and they stampeded into the path of the Elders." She cringed at what they could have done. "Luckily no one was hurt and in the distraction we managed to get away unseen." Rebaa's heart ached. "I miss my brother," she murmured.

Nen crouched beside her, some of the tension leaving her body at last. "When last see?"

Rebaa gave a weary laugh. She was so tired. She was always tired now. She had never realised carrying a child could drain one's energy so. "Many Furies ago now. It's been a long time since I've seen any of them..."

Silence. Rebaa became aware that, instead of calming further, Nen was growing agitated again. She frowned, confused. The danger was past. What was wrong now?

"How long wood sprite carry baby?"

"Eight blinks of Grindah." Rebaa answered, caught off guard by the question. "Eight black nights," she elaborated further indicating the darkest of nights when Grindah's great silver eye was fully closed.

Nen seemed to guess what she meant. Her agitation grew. "Then... baby can not be Dryad." Her black eyes were flint as they bored into Rebaa's.

Rebaa gasped as she realised her dreadful mistake. She had grown so comfortable in Nen's presence, had felt so giddy after what had just passed, she had let down her guard. The danger wasn't past. It was only just beginning.

What had she *done*?

Nen reared up to her full height. Rebaa backed away.

"You carry the Forbidden!"

Chapter Seven

The Truth

Nen was pacing up and down, her stride fierce. Rebaa eyed the entrance to the cave that had become her haven in the worst time of need. Now it was a closing trap from which she needed to escape. She wondered if she managed to flee, Nen would just let her go. She had just saved the Thal woman from the Cro after all.

"I'll leave, Nen," she said in a placating voice, though it sounded more like a plea. "I'll take the curse with me and go back to my own people."

Nen stopped her pacing and stared at her with barely concealed rage. "You not go!" she snapped. "I not let you!"

"Nen, please!" Rebaa begged. "I'm sorry I lied! I'm sorry. Just let me go!"

Nen shook her head, her broad face was haunted but determined. "No. Can't let what happened to me happen to you. No."

Nen's words halted Rebaa in her tracks, even as she edged towards escape. Her breath caught in her throat. "H-happened to you?"

Nen jabbed a finger at one of the pictures on her walls. The picture where a lone figure was being chased by those hurling rocks. "Me." She said angrily. "I birth Forbidden child."

"B-but..." Rebaa stammered, sinking heavily back to the ground, her escape forgotten. "How?"

"Cro," Nen spat. "They took everything. My life happy. Daughter of chief. People live well. Great Ones plenty. I loved strong man. He promise choose me when kill his first Great One." Nen's eyes filled with that familiar, untold pain. "Then Cro come. Cold times pushed them closer. Their spear better than our. Throw longer, kill lots of Great Ones. Take what they like."

Rebaa shuddered. She understood all too well the terror of having one's home invaded.

"Our people get hungry. Then Cro came for people, too." She turned her face away, unable to meet Rebaa's gaze. "They kill father. I tried to stop them. I angry." A mocking smile twisted her wide lips. "Better to have run. I failed. They beat me, then they hold me down." Her hands balled into fists. "Many men."

Rebaa's breath hitched as she listened to Nen's words. She had been so lucky to have been captured by Juran. If she had not fallen under his protection, she could have suffered the same fate.

"People saw," Nen continued. "They no help. Alok, my chosen one, turned his back. I dirty now. Our mighty Eron forbid breeding with the Children of his sisters and brothers. Strong lore. Forbidden act to breed with those not of people."

Rebaa nodded. She reached out tentatively to lay a comforting hand upon Nen's arm. "Achala taught this to my people, too. It is the worst trespass."

Nen put her hand over the top of Rebaa's and squeezed. "People chased me out with stones. I wounded and had to hide. I had no people now. The Cro found me and took me as slave. Nowhere else to go. Lived to do bidding. Chief made me his mate. Liked my strong. Made child. I was frightened. Not child I should have. Eron punish me with curse!" Nen paused then and Rebaa was surprised to see her anguished face brighten with a fervent light. "But then baby born. He beautiful. No curse." She tugged at her red hair. "Like mine."

Rebaa smiled through her tears. "He had hair like yours?"

Nen nodded, eyes shining with wonder for a brief moment. "I love him." She pointed to her etching of a mother and baby. "He mine. Name him Eldrax, for bear strength."

"What happened?" Rebaa asked, though she knew she probably didn't want to hear the conclusion of this doomed tale. Eldrax obviously wasn't here.

"Clan settled near great forest. South. Many dangerous animals. When Eldrax still young, chief sent on hunting trip. He too young to go!" Nen burst out, anger burning at the memory. "Hunters came back. Eldrax gone. They say boy mortal wound by big wolves, disappeared into forest. Hunters left him." Nen scraped viciously at the ground with her fingers, fury plain on her face.

"He was killed?" Rebaa whispered.

Nen flicked at a loose pebble. "No. Eron sent me miracle. Eldrax came back. He say he healed by being in forest. By Dryad." She raised her head to gaze softly at Rebaa's stunned face. "When better, he wounded Dryad in fear and escape home. Clan celebrate long. I not. What if put Eldrax in danger again? I not stand cruel life of Cro anymore. I made weapon in secret," she pointed to one of the two spears. It had carvings in the wood near the top. "I make Eron's markings of protection. I try escape. I took Eldrax. Stole out at night. I ran into warriors. I kill one but they pull Eldrax from me." She looked forlornly at her empty arms. "I forced leave him. Chased with spears. Broke lore, I tried to escape with chief child. Killed man." Nen drew a long shuddering breath. "Ran for life. Eldrax cried but could do nothing. He only child. I escaped alone. Eldrax stay with Cro."

The silence that followed was long and uncomfortable. Rebaa could not imagine the pain Nen had gone through. A thought clicked together inside her mind. "Is that why you went out after those Cro?" She asked. "You were hoping to see if Eldrax was with them." It was not a question.

Helpless tears were standing in Nen's eyes. "Yes. Every Cro clan who comes near. I frightened but I can't help. What if he there? Want to see him grown. Very much."

Rebaa placed a hand on her arm and squeezed. She tried not to imagine the horror of having to leave her baby behind in the hands of her enemies. Her free hand curled unconsciously around her belly. She vowed no-one would ever take him from her.

After the long moments of silence, Nen was able to continue her tale. "After I forced to leave child, I searched for people. Only hope. As woman, I not learn how lead hunt. Only follow. Cro women not hunt at all. I need tribe to protect, strong men. I travel long way and found people. I happy see them." Her fists tightened again. "They not happy see me. I told them no curse," she patted her belly, "but they chase me again. Chase me far. I have no people now," she said again. "I learn to hunt by self, I learn to survive. But I still alone. Eron curses me for wickedness. For bearing Forbidden."

Rebaa did not know what to say. "I'm so sorry, Nen," she whispered into the still air. Only the crackle of the fire broke the silence as the shadows flickered upon the walls, making the etchings dance and come to life. Rebaa watched them for a while with renewed sight.

When Nen could speak again, her gaze was questioning. "You have Cro baby?"

"Yes."

Nen's lips pressed into a thin line. "How you survive the curses of Cro? All sprites die when taken from trees. Get sick."

Rebaa shrugged. "My brother was learned in the skill of healing. I was able to counter their curses and survive."

Nen's eyes brightened. "How you escape them? You use Dryad magic?"

Rebaa smiled. "No, Nen, no magic."

"How?"

Rebaa still did not know if she could speak of it. The terror that so haunted her dreams. "I didn't escape," she said. "The clan chief took me for his mate, too."

Nen's face darkened. "He cruel to you?"

"No. He was good to me. He treated me gently." Rebaa choked as the memories she had so carefully buried came flooding to the surface. Memories of warm nights and the feeling of complete and utter safety. "I loved him," she confessed softly and felt her voice begin to tremble. It was too much. She straightened her back and fought the memories down. He was not coming back. He had abandoned her.

Nen rocked back at this confession. "Love? Then why you leave? Baby not accepted anywhere else."

Rebaa closed her eyes and clenched her fists to stop them trembling. She drew a deep breath. "As the Fury set in, the clan found new territory at the base of those distant mountains to the west," she said. "The ones the Cro call the Mountains of the Nine Gods. There was plenty to hunt through the cold time. The territory would have sustained us. Juran saw it as a blessing from these gods of theirs." Her voice grew soft as she got lost in the memories, seeing it all again behind her closed lids. "But the blessing turned out to be nothing more than a curse. Our hunters started disappearing in the woods around the mountains. They would go in to find game and not return. Those few who did lost their wits and would not speak of the nightmare. They would only say the woods were haunted by giant monsters that feasted on the flesh of men." Rebaa opened her eyes to stare starkly at the fire. "That left Juran with a choice. He had to risk moving the clan to find another hunting ground or stand and defeat the threat to his people. He could not tolerate such a neighbour. With the Furies getting longer and harder, Juran decided he could not give up the gift of his gods so easily, not with his son so close to being born. He decided to fight." Rebaa picked up a stray twig and threw it sharply into the fire, watching it sizzle and spit. "It was a mistake. The clan was destroyed by the enemy that came from the woods."

Nen blanched. "What could kill Cro?"

Rebaa fixed her with a dark gaze. "Creatures from the blackest nightmare, Nen. I cannot speak of them. Not even now lest I rouse their spirits. I pray to Achala that you never see such things."

Nen shivered and hid her unease by refueling the fire, brightening the cave and driving back the sudden chill.

"Your Juran not survive," she guessed.

Rebaa's eyes burned traitorously. "No. He got me out, hid me in the foothills and told me to go, to get as far away as I could." She could still see his green eyes as he beseeched her to leave him and run. "He promised me he would follow. He promised. But he betrayed me. He went back to his people and was slaughtered with them. He left me alone with the curse of his Forbidden child." She realised she was crying openly now, in grief, in anger. Her carefully built walls were crumbling around her, too weak to contain what was inside.

Nen was thoughtful. "He clan chief?"

Rebaa nodded once through her tears, not trusting her voice as she fought to regain control.

"Then he could not leave people. Dishonor to soul in Cro lore."

"I don't care about honour!" Rebaa burst out. "I want him with me! Why did he have to go back?!"

Nen was silent. After a moment she simply reached out and pulled Rebaa to her, holding her close against the thick brown furs. At first, Rebaa fought to pull away. She could not give in! She had to stay strong! But Nen held her firm and as the Thal woman began to stroke her hair, Rebaa could fight no longer. With a wail, she succumbed to the grief she had been holding so tightly in check and poured out her loss and pain in the comfort and safety of Nen's arms. She didn't know if she would ever stop.

"Maybe only way to save you and child," Nen murmured quietly to her. "Maybe had to go so you could live." She continued to stroke Rebaa's dark hair. "Must forgive. He save you. Must find *shalanaki.*"

"I don't know if I can," Rebaa choked. "Not yet. Maybe someday I might. If we survive."

"You say must go back to people?" Nen questioned. "No go. They hate you. They kill you. Will not accept curse. I try. Got stoned."

"He left me with no choice, Nen!" Rebaa flared. "I need a people. I have to go back. I have nowhere else to go."

"Do," Nen said, voice firm. She held Rebaa out at arm's length. "Can stay. I look after. We look after. You outcast, I outcast. I hunt, you protect us with knowledge of Great Spirit. We take care of baby."

Rebaa fell silent, stunned by the words. Her thoughts buzzed stupidly. She stared into Nen's determined eyes. The black gaze did not waver and very slowly a new hope began to stir. She chewed her lip, thinking. If she stayed, she would never see her brother again. She longed to see him. She missed her people with all her heart. But Nen was right. They would never accept her back. She had only set out to find them because she had had no other hope. Now she did have another hope. She had only turned down Nen's previous offer of sanctuary because she felt sure Nen would kill her once she found out the truth about her baby. That fear was no longer valid. Nen had shared in her plight. Indeed, they were outcasts together.

At that precise moment the baby kicked fervently.

"Ah!" Rebaa protested at the abuse. He was so strong!

Without warning, Nen placed a warm hand on her belly, feeling the kicks under her large palm. Her dark eyes melted into a loving reverence. "No fear, little *juaan,*" she whispered. "I be your *tarhe.*" The baby quieted under her touch.

"Tarhe?" Rebaa asked.

"Protector Mother," Nen answered solemnly. "Sacred vow. I pledge my life to baby. Mark of family in Thal tribe."

Tears began to slide down Rebaa's cheeks once more but, this time, she did not taste the bitterness of grief. "Oh, Nen."

"Stay?" Nen's eyes bored into hers.

Rebaa sobbed and threw her arms around Nen's shoulders. "Yes. I'll stay with you. Thank you. Thank you so much."

Rebaa was home.

Chapter Eight

Birth

Her dreams were easier that night and she rested fully for the first time in a long time. Having finally poured out her grief to Nen, Rebaa somehow felt lighter. She had taken the first step on her path to recovery. Maybe one day she would be able to make peace with Juran.

When Achala dawned, Nen and Rebaa moved the bodies of the Cro men that had been crushed by the stampede. It wasn't pleasant work but they could not leave the bodies in the open to attract unwanted attention. They pulled them into a shallow ravine as far away from the cave as they could get them and then piled rocks on top of the bloody corpses. Rebaa had to wash in the stream for a long time after that.

Time slid by in a contented haze. By day Rebaa helped Nen with the everyday chores of keeping the cave clean and habitable and stocked with anything they may need. They still had plenty of bear meat left to last, so there was no need to hunt for more. Nen made Rebaa new clothes and also coverings for the baby ready for when he arrived. Rebaa was very touched by this. To complete her work and using the last of the bear skin, Nen fashioned a warm sling that would enable Rebaa to carry the baby next to her heart while still being able to move unhindered. All this waited in a warm corner of the cave ready for when it would be called for.

This life Rebaa had found with Nen might not be what she had imagined her life to be, so far from her people and their forests, living in the shadows of the mountains inside a cave with a Thal woman, but she was as happy as she could be. Accepted. She and her unborn. They were safe. She could not ask for more than that.

Rebaa waddled uncomfortably in the pale morning light behind Nen as they walked to the mountain stream to drink. Her back was aching. It had ached all through the latter stages of her pregnancy. Juran's child was big. Bigger than the average Achalaja child, Rebaa would like to guess, and it had put extra strains upon her small body. Today, however, it was harder to bear. The ache was almost unbearable.

She gasped suddenly and had to sit down on a rock as the baby gave a particularly strong kick. It felt like he was doing somersaults. So close. She felt a shiver of apprehension. She hoped everything went smoothly with the birth. She had no healers or old medicine women to help her if things went wrong.

Nen paused when she realised Rebaa wasn't following. Her concern was evident on her face. Rebaa tried to smile reassuringly. She rubbed her sore side. She felt so cumbersome. "It's ok, Nen. He's just kicking like a horse."

"Ah," the shadows in the Thal's eyes eased. She smiled. "Little *juaan*."

"What does that mean?" Rebaa was curious.

"It mean 'strong one' in my tribe."

"Strong one," Rebaa repeated. She rubbed her belly again ruefully. "He certainly is."

They drank their fill and started to make their way back to the cave. The birds were singing in the air. Rebaa recognised them all. All except one. There was a repeated chirrup that she just couldn't place. Strange. It was answered by another strange call coming from further away. Rebaa listened intently but the unfamiliar bird fell silent. She shrugged it off. All manner of creatures were being displaced by the increasing cold and the ever encroaching Fury Wastes. She had better get used to seeing and hearing strange things.

By the time they reached the cave, the wind was picking up strongly, gathering loose snow on its icy breath and swirling it into their faces. Rebaa shivered. A storm was coming. Squinting, she saw clouds gathering on the horizon. Nen sniffed the air. "Bad."

Rebaa agreed. She could feel the changes in the air pressure. "We better gather more firewood before it hits. If it lingers, we might need it." They could not afford to let that fire to go out.

Nen pointed further down the slope. "Wood not far. Plenty of branches."

Rebaa pressed her hands into her aching back and groaned. This was the last thing she needed but continued heat was vital to their survival. It had to be done. "Lead the way," she told Nen.

The wood turned out to be a sparse copse tucked away in a shallow dell. Together, they collected as many fallen twigs and branches as they could carry and climbed back up to the cave to deposit their loads beside their idling fire to dry. Rebaa assessed the wood piles with a sinking heart. It would take a couple more trips to build up a satisfactory supply.

They were traveling down the slope for a second time when Rebaa heard the strange bird call again. "Do you know what bird that is?" she asked Nen out of mild interest as she struggled down the bank.

Nen listened with an intent frown. "No," she said finally. "Never heard before."

"Nor have I," Rebaa said. "I wonder-"

Whatever she was about to say was abruptly cut off as the base of her back contracted in sudden pain.

"Ah!" she gasped, stumbling and catching herself on her hands.

Nen was there in an instant. "What wrong?"

"I don't know," Rebaa panted, a little wild eyed. Her dirty hands went to her belly.

Nen's hands fluttered over her. "Get back home. Get rest."

"Yes," Rebaa agreed, struggling to her feet, only to sink back down when another wave of pain hit home. That was when she felt her waters break. "Ah!" she gasped again. She grabbed Nen's arm. "Nen, he's coming! The baby is coming now!"

"Quick." Nen stooped and pulled her arm over her shoulder, helping to keep her steady. She half carried Rebaa back up the slope. The Thal woman was more than a little anxious. Rebaa's heart was beating quickly, sick with apprehension. She had witnessed many births and none of them had looked exactly pleasant. She was more frightened than she was willing to admit. She clutched on to Nen with all her strength as another contraction rippled through her, the pain was moving round to the front. It seemed to take forever to get back to the cave. Rebaa heard the bird cry again, closer this time. She wished it would shut up, its strangeness was more an irritation now than a curiosity.

At last, they were back inside the cave. Nen piled up some furs and laid Rebaa down upon them. She stoked and refueled the fire then looked for other things to fuss with. Failing that, she fidgeted where she stood. "What now?" she asked.

"We just have to wait, I suppose," Rebaa said shakily. "Just talk to me. I'm… frightened."

Nen offered her hand as another powerful contraction rocked Rebaa's small frame. She could not help the cry of agony that pulled from her lips. This was going to be bad.

Nen stroked back her hair and murmured comfortingly to her, her voice flowing out in a steady stream. She lapsed into her own tongue for ease and Rebaa could not understand her words. It did not matter, just the rhythm of the Thal woman's husky voice was enough to sooth her and give her something solid to cling to. She knew she could depend on Nen to help her through this. Whatever happened.

The day grew late. The blizzard that had been promised swept in. Rebaa could not see very far out of the cave. The falling snow obscured everything beyond the first few rocks. The wind, unfortunately, was blowing directly inside. It bit at Rebaa's fevered brow and she shivered violently before breaking off into another keening wail of pain, her belly drawing tight. Would this never end?!

Nen left her side briefly. Rebaa reached after her in desperation, not wanting to be left alone. Nen quieted her and then began piling rocks in the cave's entrance. She had a sufficient amount to block the opening and break the howling wind. She left holes at the top so the smoke from their fire could still escape.

Night had fallen completely when Rebaa's contractions reached fever pitch. She could hardly regain her breath between one and the next. She was screaming, begging for it to stop. Nen was beside herself.

It was when Rebaa felt sure she was going to die, that a howl from the outside split the air. Her blood turned to ice at the sound of it.

For it was not the voice of the wind.

Rebaa's wild, rolling eyes turned towards the blocked entrance. "Oh no," she whimpered through her tears and struggles. "No, not now!" Senses heightened in this most vulnerable of moments, Rebaa felt them approach. She felt clearly every single thought and intent. They were being hunted.

"Nen!" she grabbed the Thal woman's arm, fighting through yet another wave of pain. "They're back. The Cro. They've come back for us!" She fell back on her elbows, crying out.

Fierce shouts rose above the storm outside, getting closer. More bird calls went up and more answered, swelling the numbers. Only, those calls had never come from any bird. Rebaa raged against her own stupidity. They had been being watched the entire time. Now the Cro were ready to exact their revenge. They couldn't have timed it more perfectly.

Fighting for concentration, Rebaa searched the energies of the earth outside, hoping for something, anything. There was nothing. All life had gone into hiding to wait out the storm. Maybe that too had been a part of the Cro's design. Rebaa was helpless. Their cunning never ceased to amaze her. Sweat poured from her brow along with bitter tears. She had failed her son. Failed him before he had even taken his first breath.

Nen sat stiffly beside her, face dark and grim as the shouts intensified. Their enemy knew they were getting close to their target. The Thal woman stared down at Rebaa, convulsing in the throes of child birth, then she turned her face to the walled entrance, then back to Rebaa again. A hard determination set in her eyes. She knelt and put her hands on Rebaa's belly. "*Gor cha tarhe, ki juaan,*" she murmured softly.

She stood up, drawing away from Rebaa, her face fierce. What Rebaa read in her eyes sent her into a panic.

"Nen?" she asked desperately, already knowing the terrible answer. "Where are you going?! Stay with me!"

Nen shook her head. "I vow *tarhe,* for little strong one," she said quietly. "If I stay, they find us. I go. Can lead them away. Maybe in snow, can escape. Only hope." She moved to pick up her spear. She laid the second at Rebaa's side. The one inscribed with Eron's markings of protection.

"No! Nen!" Rebaa cried, gasping and trying to rise to prevent her. She fell back when her body would not obey. "Nen! Please. Stay with me! I need you! We just have to stay quiet. Maybe they'll miss us in the storm." She was frantic.

Again, Nen shook her head. She was already moving for the cave entrance. "Know where cave is. I have go. Protect baby." She began pulling rocks away from the blocked entrance, just enough for her to slip out into the fractious, stormy night. "Only one who can."

"No! Nen!" Rebaa shrieked. But Nen had already begun piling the rocks back into place behind her. She met Rebaa's eyes across the space between them before replacing the last. The moment stretched as they stared into each others' faces. One pleading, the other resolute.

"*Shalanaki*, Rebaa," Nen whispered, then the last rock slid into place and she was gone.

"Nooooo!" Rebaa howled in despair. "Nen! Come back!" But she could think no more as she felt the baby begin to arrive and she had to heave with all her might, instinct driving her to do what she must. The pain went on and on. She doubted that if all of her bones had been broken at once, she could have felt this much pain. Through it all, she kept her teeth stubbornly locked together. She would not scream. She would not make it easy for those beasts to find her. The cries outside faded into the distance. Nen was leading them away. *Nen...*

Finally, in blood and fire and in the loneliness of the night, Rebaa's son was born.

Chapter Nine

Shalanaki

Exhausted, Rebaa collapsed back, gasping. Sweat dripped from her brow. She trembled all over, too weak to even to raise her head. But then the cries of her new born reached her ears. Finding a strength she did not know she had, Rebaa pulled herself upright and scooped up her baby from where he lay struggling, naked and helpless. Quickly, she grabbed the sharpened rock that Nen had used for stripping skins. With shaking fingers, she held it in the fire for a few moments then used it to slice through the bluish rope that still tied her baby to her. She knew there was more to come but she would just have to wait.

Numb, Rebaa gathered her squalling infant and wrapped him inside her furs next to her breast. With the tears still falling from the trauma of his birth and her fear for Nen, she looked down into his face for the very first time. He was wailing lustily, protesting hard at being brought into this strange and cold world. He was whole and strong. To her relief, he showed none of the cursed deformities that had begun to mark so many Achalaja newborns. His piercing wails continued. Rebaa glanced fearfully at the blocked cave entrance. They might hear him. They'd come and they'd kill him. Nen's efforts would be for nothing.

"Shh, shh," she put her face close to his, touching at his new and undeveloped mind. "You must be quiet. We must not be found." She was still shaking violently.

The baby stopped squalling. He opened his eyes and blinked at her. Rebaa gasped. Green eyes. Juran's eyes. His son. Blinking back tears, she gazed down into that serious little face and was knocked breathless with a love that transcended everything else she had ever felt. She wondered dimly that the ground did not tremble at the strength of it. Nothing else mattered now but him. She would die for him if she had to.

The wind lashed against the rocks piled against the cave mouth, whistling eerily through the cracks. Rebaa wrapped her arms around her precious one, rocking back and forth while her tears fell. She waited for Nen to return. She refused to believe she would not. Nen knew what she was doing. She knew this range. The snow would've hidden her enough to evade their enemies once she had lead them away. Rebaa repeated this to herself over and over as she continued to hold her son and remain quiet, waiting for her friend to return.

The wind eventually blew itself out. Rebaa found the silence it left behind worse than the wailing. She fed her new baby and saw to it all that had followed him from the birth was burned, lest it attract predators. She cleaned him and dressed him in the warm coverings Nen had made, all the while hoping to feel at any moment the return of a familiar presence and the soft tread in the snow outside.

It never came.

It was the longest night Rebaa had ever spent. The growing anxiety gripped at her heart like claws, making it hard to breathe. The empty moments slipped by. She knew now that something was wrong. She wanted to go out and find Nen but she would not take her baby out into danger and the exposure of the night. Still she waited, breathless but with a steadily dying hope.

At last the dawn light reached its fingers through the gaps in the rocks and brushed across Rebaa's sleepless face. She and her baby were still alone. She could wait no longer. Donning the sling Nen had fashioned out of the bear hide, she tucked her baby into it, making sure he was as protected as possible. She moved stiffly. The birth had taken a severe toll. Blood dripped down her leg and she knew she was torn. She hissed softly at the pain of every motion. It didn't matter. She had to find Nen. Seizing the spear her friend had left for her, she cast quickly about with her higher senses. She felt nothing. No living thing was anywhere near the cave. Rebaa shuddered at the thought. *Nen!* Her heart cried out. *Please don't leave me alone!*

With shaking hands, she pushed hard at the rocks blocking the entrance to the cave. She didn't have the patience to take them down one by one. They tumbled outward with a noisy clatter. After so long of keeping such careful silence, the sudden din was frightening. Rebaa froze, fully expecting an attack at any moment.

Nothing happened and after a while, Rebaa made herself move again. The cold hit her like a fist, stealing her breath. The rocky landscape tumbling away before her was stark and empty. Only the tall, dead grasses stirred in the breeze above the thick blanket of snow. She was alone. Wearily and leaning heavily on her spear to aid her aching body, Rebaa set out to find what she would.

"Nen!" she called out as often as she dared, listening hard, each time hopeful that she would hear a faint answer floating over the deadening snow. "Nen!"

She trudged for what felt like an eternity, she had to stop often to catch her breath and feed her baby. She was weak. She needed rest but she could not stop until she found her friend. What if Nen had fallen and was injured, unable to walk? What if she was trapped somewhere, waiting patiently for Rebaa to come? The image was a torment. Rebaa could not abandon her. She *had* to find her. Whatever awaited, she had to know.

Darkness was once again creeping over the snowy land when Rebaa at last detected the brush of a presence in the near distance. It was a faint energy, flickering like a flame fighting to stay alight against a relentless wind. Rebaa struggled to increase her pace, bracing herself on her spear and clutching her baby close with her other arm. He was very quiet.

Scrambling over the rough ground, Rebaa cried out when she spotted something orange billowing gently in the breeze above the dead grasses and scattered rocks. A vivid and terribly familiar shade of orange. Everything in the surrounding area was spotted and spattered with deep crimson.

Rebaa's stride faltered. She did not want to witness the scene that must await her just beyond those rocks. Her heart crumbled in her chest even as she forced herself to move forward, hot and cold all over. She knew what was there. She knew it.

Rebaa sobbed and fell to her knees beside the body of her friend. Nen was lying partially naked in a pool of blood. The sickly scent filled Rebaa's nostrils. Wounds littered the pale body. Nen's stained spear had rolled away from her hand. Rebaa noticed two other bodies lying nearby. Nen had managed to kill some of her enemies before they overcame her.

"Nen!" Rebaa sobbed, blinded by tears. "Nen!" She feared she was already too late and Nen had left her.

But the black eyes opened slightly and Nen turned her head towards the sound of Rebaa's voice. "Rebaa..." she slurred.

"Yes, I-I'm here, Nen, I'm here. You're going to be alright, you're s-safe now." She caught hold of one of the thick hands between her own. It was freezing. With trembling fingers, Rebaa did her best to cover her friend with the tattered and torn furs.

"Baby?" the eyes opened slightly wider, a fear and a fervent hope flickering in their fading depths.

"He's here, Nen," Rebaa soothed quickly. "He's here, he wants to meet you, his *tarhe*." She lifted the baby out of his sling and put him near Nen's face so she could see him fully. She was desperate to keep the Thal woman conscious. She had to find a way to save her. What would her brother do? She would have given anything for Barias to be near. "He's safe. You saved us."

The dark eyes glimmered as Nen focused them with obvious effort on the baby before her. He stared back solemnly and then reached out to touch her cheek. Nen smiled slightly and caught his tiny hand in hers. "Good... Saved little strong one."

Rebaa could feel her life energy slipping away quickly now. The bright flame was giving up its battle against the relentless wind. "Stay with me, Nen," Rebaa begged. "We need you still."

Nen shook her head slightly. "No. Weary. I go to Eron now." Tears started in her eyes as she fixed them on Rebaa. "You think he forgive me?"

Rebaa's own tears fell on her bruised face. "Yes, Nen," she whispered. "He'll forgive you. He'll have been proud to have had such a brave child."

Nen brushed at the baby laid close beside her. "Achala will forgive you, too," she murmured. She then grasped Rebaa's arm with surprising strength. "Promise me you look after baby," she beseeched. "Let nobody take from you. Keep him safe, even from own people. They seek to kill him. Don't let them."

"Never," Rebaa swore fiercely, her eyes burning. She scooped her son from where he lay and clutched him to her as if to keep him forever by her heart. "No one will ever hurt him," she promised. "They will have to kill me first!"

A faint smile touched Nen's pale lips and a quiet peace fell over her face. "Good. Do what I could not or live with pain all of life. Protect baby..." Her eyes drifted closed.

"No." Rebaa gripped the slack hand. The flame was now an ember. "Nen," she shook the hand. "Nen?"

"*Shalanaki,* Rebaa." The whisper faded on the breeze.

Rebaa could barely speak the words. "*Shalanaki,* Nen."

And she was gone. The ember smouldered and went out.

Rebaa sat there holding her friend's hand, keeping her company as she passed into the next journey. Rebaa prayed it would be a happier path than the one Nen had travelled in this most cruel and unforgiving world. Rebaa kept her vigil until darkness fell around them.

"*Shalanaki,* Nen."

Chapter Ten

Decision

Rebaa did not know how long she crouched over Nen's body, wailing her grief to the sky. Unheeding of her torment, Achala had dipped below the horizon, leaving her alone and in darkness. Alone. She was very much alone now.

Finally, her tears ran out. Her eyes were red and swollen and her throat was raw. There was no more she could do. Nen was gone. The cold began to suck at her. Stiffly, she rose to her feet. With deadened eyes, she stared down at the lifeless body of the one who had offered hope and acceptance for her and her Forbidden offspring. Both were stolen from her now. All hope was as dead as the cold form lying before her.

Rebaa did not have the strength to move Nen to a better place. Numbly, she began to gather rocks and pile them over her friend's body, protecting it from all that would come along. She was tired, in pain, but she did not stop until her task was done. Her frozen fingers were raw by the time she had finished. As a final touch, she scratched a shining circle into one of the highest stones. She had no idea if the Thals possessed a symbol for their Eron but she hoped the mark of Achala would offer some protection to Nen as she slept.

The bodies of the Cro she left to rot without mark and kept her back turned on them disdainfully. Wolves howled on the darkening horizon. Their cries held a hungry note as the scent of blood drifted to them on the wind. Rebaa smiled grimly. She gazed down at the pile of rocks that marked her dear friend's final resting place. Her face was now dry. She had no more tears. Gracing Nen with one last gesture of farewell, Rebaa stumbled away.

The wolves were howling all around her as she made her way back to the cave. She did not hurry. Her face was resolute. She was Achalaja and she did not fear the wolves. All the Children of the Great Spirit would stay away from her tonight. The familiar cave opened up before her in the slope of the hill. This time, however, it offered no welcome. Exhausted, Rebaa stumbled inside. Holding her baby close, she threw herself down on the furs beside the fire and knew no more.

When she awoke, it was barely light. The cries of her baby had awoken her. He was hungry. Painfully, she sat up and fed him. While he suckled greedily, Rebaa tried to avoid looking at all the familiar objects in the cave that had become her home. The piled rocks, the furs, the rock drawings. The fire was smouldering but she could not bring herself to rebuild it. All served only to remind her of Nen and the life that had now been stolen from her.

She swallowed back her tears, casting her eyes down at her baby, letting him ground her. She would have to leave. This was no longer the sanctuary that it had once been. The Cro must know that they had not finished what they came to do. They had seen two women challenge them the day they had found the bear. One death had satisfied their need for revenge the previous night. How long would it be until the need for a second death drove them to hunt once more?

It was no longer safe. Rebaa had to get her baby far from here. But where? She closed her eyes. She was confronted with the very same dilemma she had faced before she ever met Nen. It seemed she had never really escaped her fate. It had simply been sitting, waiting for her.

She thought again of her own people as she looked down into her son's green eyes. They stared trustingly back at her. Rebaa burst into tears. There was no way she could make them believe he was an Achalaja child. If his size did not betray him, his damning eyes certainly would. No Achalaja had eyes of that colour. What would they do to him? She rocked her baby back and forth, despairing and undecided.

She could try to throw herself on the mercy of another Cro clan. They might accept the little one but Juran's fearsome reputation had been far reaching. She could not risk another clan recognising Juran's mate. They would kill her on the spot. And the baby. No. She could be less sure of that unpredictable and bloodthirsty race than she could of her own. She shuddered.

At least if she went home, the love of her brother may be enough to protect her. Maybe. It was a faint glimmer in the darkness and she had to cling to that. There was nothing else.

All that was left to do was to prepare for a long journey. It would take her many rises and falls of Achala to reach the borders of her old forest home. Despite her apprehension of facing her people again after so long, facing them with the greatest of sins, part of her longed to be surrounded by the protective strength of the trees again. In all the time she had spent away, she had never really gotten used to the feeling of nakedness out on the open plains. It was unnatural to her.

Getting to her feet, Rebaa began to gather what she would need. She picked up one of Nen's leather carriers and slung it around her body opposite her baby's sling. Moving to the entrance of the cave, she filled the carrier with the hunks of frozen meat Nen had stored outside in the snow. Next, she picked up the pieces of flint needed to spark a fire and stowed them on top of the meat.

Lastly, she collected Nen's spear. Her beloved friend's final gift. She could not use it to hunt but she could use it as a crutch to aid her ragged body. She had still not recovered from the birth of her baby. She was really in no condition to travel. She was weak and her birthing wounds had not fully healed. She was not even strong enough to mend herself. It was not a promising start but to stay here meant certain death. She had to take her chances and hope her body did not fail before her journey was complete. Her baby was depending on her.

That last thought gave her strength and Rebaa stood straight and fierce, setting her will. She glanced around the cave for one last time. A picture on the wall caught her eye and she reached out to trace the etching of a mother and child. It was a gesture of farewell. Swallowing her tears, Rebaa dropped her hand and strode determinedly out into the open air. She did not look back.

The fire smouldered behind her and died.

Chapter Eleven

The Will to Survive

The days that followed her departure from the cave blurred together in a never ending torture. Exhaustion, hunger, fear, cold, pain. That was all there was. Still Rebaa kept going. She must travel south and not stop until she had reached the forests of her ancestors. She had to get there. She had to. The whole time she remained alert for signs of pursuit. If the Cro picked up her trail, all her efforts would be for nothing.

By night she tried desperately to strike a fire for warmth but she failed each time. She had never truly mastered the skill and the fuel she gathered was always wet with snow. She had no means to dry it. The snow thinned the further south she travelled but the conditions became no less fierce. She stumbled through the nights, fearful to sleep lest she succumb to the elements and never wake up again.

When she was finally forced to rest, she clung to her baby and cried out her grief for all the loss in her life. For Juran, for Nen. Both had died to save her. Both had left her alone. Only her baby's warmth against her heart gave her the strength to stagger back to her feet each time and keep going. Nothing else mattered but him.

Stains of blood marked Rebaa's every resting place.

She starved. With no fire, she could not cook the meat she had brought. Her baby, however, had a voracious appetite and he sapped what little strength she had left. She had to eat something otherwise she would not be capable of feeding him. In the end, she became so desperate that she ate hunks of meat raw, fighting down her revulsion so as not to bring it back up again. She had no choice. Survival was all that mattered. If she died, her baby died. But as the days and nights passed, the meat, thawed by her body heat, began to smell and turn bad. She had no means to cure it. Rebaa was finally forced to drop her now useless load. She continued to walk. And walk, the blood of her wounds dripping a crimson trail behind her. Carrion birds began to wheel overhead. Rebaa hissed her defiance to their watchful waiting and struggled on.

Birds, however, were not the worst creatures to stalk these lands. A couple of days later, Rebaa detected a distant presence on the very edges of her awareness that told her something far more deadly had begun to haunt her footsteps. Her worst fears had been realised.

The Cro had picked up her trail.

What hope she had left fled. She was dying, she was still far from home and now she was being pursued. The knowledge crushed her. If she had ever needed a miracle, it was now. Rebaa leaned against a tree and turned her face to the sky. Achala was hidden behind the roving clouds. "Please," she whispered to the unseen face. "I know I have done wrong. I know I have shamed and betrayed you in the most terrible way but please let me save my baby. He is innocent. He does not know. Give me strength, most sacred Achala. Let me reach my people before my enemies catch me."

Achala did not answer. She kept her face hidden and turned from Rebaa. Rebaa lowered her eyes. There would be no miracle. Achala had indeed abandoned her. She looked down into her baby's face. He stared back solemnly. Somehow he seemed to understand that his mother was in trouble. He reached out with one little curled hand and patted her cheek. His green eyes were very determined.

Rebaa laughed and sobbed at the same time. "You think we can make it?" she asked softly. The green eyes held steady. Rebaa nodded. He at least, had not abandoned her. "Alright, then, we'll make it together. You and me, little strong one. Let's go home."

Rebaa pushed away from the tree, wove a little on her feet as the world swam before her eyes, then she found her balance and plunged on into the frost-hardened landscape. She increased her pace, keeping an eye on the energies flickering like wildfire behind her. She had to stay ahead. But even with her increased pace, she knew they were gaining steadily. She could not keep this up for long.

Finally, as all hope dwindled and Achala rose on yet another day, Rebaa crested a low rise and a dark line along the horizon rose before her blurring vision. The forests of her birth place stood awaiting before her.

Tears sprang to Rebaa's eyes. "We did it!" she rasped to her sleeping baby as he dozed next to her heart. "We made it." Overcome, Rebaa stumbled forward, leaning heavily on her spear. She was home at last!

She was so distracted by her triumph and exhaustion, she failed to watch for the enemies that had gained so quickly on her from behind.

A faint shout her made her spin around with a cry on her lips. She fought to focus her failing eyes as she stared back in the direction she had come. She could just make out five figures standing on the crests of the hills behind.

Rebaa snarled in fierce defiance to the tall, lithe forms silhouetted on the horizon. Even after all she had gone through, they were never going to let her rest. They would pursue her until the very last step. She had no doubt they could see her now. She could see them and she was in the open on white, frosty ground. She stood out like a black ox in the middle of a plain.

She turned back to stare at the distant border of the great forest. She was closer to that than the Cro were to her. They would have to travel twice the distance to catch her. If she could get into the trees, she knew she would be safe. Five Cro would not dare follow her into Achalaja territory.

The world narrowed down to this one breathless moment as Rebaa assessed her chances. She was closer to her goal but she knew the Cro could travel twice as fast as she could. They also had the advantage of not currently dying on their feet. This would be a fairly even race.

Rebaa's mouth set into a grim line. She had not survived all that she had just to fall now! She faced her pursuers up on the hills and cried out her defiance once more. She was going home! Gathering her most precious bundle to her, Rebaa turned and ran for her life.

The chase was joined. Hunting cries sounded behind as the Cro threw themselves after her in pursuit.

Rebaa pounded across the expanse between her and the protection of the trees. Her breath soon came in short, laboured gasps. Her legs burned. The injury from the bear began to make itself known, causing her to limp. Her baby became a rock weight in her arms. Already she was slowing. Still she ran, the tree line growing larger and larger with each ragged step. Her heart pounded painfully in her chest.

The eager voices grew louder behind. They were gaining, gaining. She felt their murderous energy bearing unstoppably down upon her.

Go, go! She chanted to herself. *Run! Not far now!*

She was almost there, only fifty strides away. She was stumbling now. Completely and utterly spent. She did not know what strength kept her on her legs. She pushed herself on. Nearly there.

A harsh voice and the sound of pounding feet directly behind her told her she was too late. She was not close enough. One of them was faster than the rest and he was right behind her. She felt him reaching out in triumph, his fingers about to brush her back and bring their deadly chase to its violent end.

Rebaa acted. Screaming with rage, she wheeled around. For the first time she became acutely aware of the spear she somehow still clutched in her hand. Without thinking she stopped and braced herself, holding the point of the spear out and up, its butt against the ground. The startled Cro did not have time to halt his momentum. He drove himself upon the sharpened tip that waited for him, his weight thrusting him forward, deeper and deeper until it pierced his very heart. Wide blue eyes stared in shock at Rebaa as he coughed up blood, gurgling wordlessly. Then the life faded and he tumbled to the ground, dead.

Gasping, Rebaa stared at him, frozen with revulsion and disbelief before shouts of fury from the dead Cro's companions shook her back to reality. Leaving the spear embedded in her enemy's chest, she spun and fled for the trees, leaping at last through the protective line just as a poorly aimed spear seared past her ear and bounced off an unyielding trunk.

Rebaa continued to run until she was a safe distance into the woods. Finally, she had to stop and leaned heavily against a tree. She listened to the curses and shouts of frustration behind her but no sounds of pursuit reached her pounding ears. She had been right. So small a band would not dare violate these borders.

She had made it. She had… The pounding in her ears became a roar. The world turned and Rebaa stumbled, clutching at the tree. She felt her heart beat unsteadily in her chest. That last effort had been too much for her failing body. The trees blurred before her eyes. She shook her head to clear it of the growing darkness. She could not die now! Her baby still needed her! It was not safe. But the darkness did not heed her will and it continued to grow. Boneless, Rebaa slid down against the tree. She was losing the battle. Wrapping her arms protectively around her baby, she held him tight. She would not let him go! He was the last thing she thought of before endless darkness enveloped her.

Chapter Twelve

Promise

"...what happened to her?"

Voices. The voices were coming from all around. She had no sense of her body apart from the weight against her chest. She had no idea where she was or what was happening but knew she must hold on to that weight. It was important.

"...don't know. The wolves dragged her in..."

"What is she dressed in?" came another disgusted voice. "She wears the garb of accursed flesh-eating ground-dwellers!" Someone spat.

The words sounded strange to her ears. It took long moments for her to realise the reason. She had not heard this tongue spoken in...

"She's nearly dead," a familiar voice spoke near her head, shaking with suppressed emotion. She felt fingers brushing her temples. "She's barely there. Let me look at her!"

Barias? She wanted to speak but she could not gain the control needed. She drifted again. The scents of winter trees, earth and leaf mould were strong in her nostrils. She clung to that sense.

"What's that she's holding?" came yet another voice.

"It's a baby," somebody else said.

"It doesn't feel right. What *is* it?!" the tone became fearful, filled with dread and hardening certainty. "Barias, move out of the way!"

Someone began to pull at the weight she held so firmly in her unfeeling arms. It began to cry. That roused her and she felt a little bit of her physical awareness return. Pain washed over her.

"It's a monster!" somebody exclaimed. "Get it away from her. Look at its eyes! In the name of Achala, I will end this curse!"

Someone tried to drag the warm weight in her arms away from her. It cried louder in distress. They were hurting it! Full awareness rushed back to Rebaa like a bolt of lightening.

"No!" she shrieked, pulling her baby back and throwing herself protectively over the top of him. "Get away from him!" Her words were half Cro out of habit but her meaning was clear.

Her vision swirled dangerously. She saw a leaf-clad figure before her, a large rock raised threateningly between his hands.

"Get away!" she hissed fiercely, curling her body around her baby. If they wanted him, they would have to kill her, too!

Angry muttering broke out as Rebaa fought to stay awake, braced over her newborn. She had to stay awake. His very life hung in the balance.

"Unnatural."

"Accursed!"

"Forbidden."

"Forbidden!"

The words buzzed like angry bees from all around her and she was in the midst of the nest. Emotions were fanning quickly into a fierce unstoppable wildfire.

"It cannot be allowed to exist. It will bring an end to us all!" Their combined determination set on one terrible course of action. "It must die."

Rebaa began to cry. "Barias!" she sobbed, unfocused eyes searching for her brother. "Help me. Don't let them!" But he did not step forward. He did not come to her aid. The anger continued to grow. Her sobs grew desperate. All this way, all that suffering and she had still lost. Her one hope evaporated into nothingness. No one was going to defend her. Not even her brother. She had made the wrong choice. She had broken her promise to Nen. She could not keep her baby safe. Her eyes screwed shut, tightening her arms. She would at least hold on as long as she could...

"Get away from that girl!" a voice cracked out over the din. "Let me through!" It was a female voice and it rang with a terrifying authority. Rebaa felt a power moving toward her such as she had not felt in a long time. She had forgotten. She heard the crackling of leaves as many feet shuffled hastily backwards. Then thin, cool fingers were brushing her brow.

"Easy, young one." The voice said. "You are safe now."

Safe? How could she be safe? She was never safe. Rebaa blinked up into the face so close beside hers. It was an ancient visage, deeply lined and framed with long, white hair. A face filled with endless wisdom and lavender eyes that burned with the energy of the Great Spirit himself.

"Sefaan," she rasped in recognition. Her tribe's Kamaali. A Seeress of the Spirit. The sacred Guide to her people. The very last of her kind.

"Sefaan!" Another female voice snapped. "She cannot stay here. Not if she refuses to give up that thing. It condemns us all in the eyes of Achala. It is Forbidden!"

Sefaan stood straight and faced the speaker. "Very well, Aardn," she spoke cuttingly. "If you insist. But know that if you cast this girl from our trees, I will accompany her."

Gasps of shock rippled around the tribe. Rebaa saw the red-gold faces and varying shades of indigo eyes fill with doubt and fear. They shifted uncertainly. The choice Sefaan had faced them with was unthinkable. Keep the abomination or risk losing the voice of the Great Spirit for their tribe.

"We cannot keep it, Sefaan," Aardn's voice now held a desperate edge. "It's a monster! It puts everybody at risk. There is a reason such things are Forbidden!"

Sefaan regarded her steadily. "It is only a baby for now, Aardn. You must indeed have grown weak in your old age to fear an infant." Her words struck at the Elder's pride. "A child cannot hurt us. We will watch him closely. Once he is old enough to survive on his own, you may send him on his way. Until then, he must stay with Rebaa under her protection. And mine." She added as an after threat. The silence was deafening. Not even the birds dared to speak a sound.

Rebaa could not believe what she was hearing. She began to tremble all over, the world swirling dangerously. She could not hold herself together any longer.

"Barias!" she heard Sefaan snap at her brother. "Don't just stand there. Heal her. She's dying!"

A soft tread, then Rebaa felt hands against her head and tears dripping on her face as her brother's energy flowed into her. She latched on to it greedily as she felt him work. His skill in the healing art was unsurpassed. Her pain eased almost immediately. She drifted in and out of consciousness, never letting go of her baby until she heard Barias whisper in a broken voice. "She will live now. Her wounds are healed but she needs food and much rest."

"Good," Sefaan murmured then her voice rose to address the rest of the tribe. "Swear to me that you will honour my word," the Kamaali pressed. "No one will attempt to harm this girl or her offspring. Not until the time comes for him to leave." The silence stretched. "Swear it!" Sefaan's power radiated out, lashing at them.

It was Aardn who finally spoke for the tribe, voice heavy with unwilling defeat. "It seems you have left us with little choice, Sefaan. We swear."

Rebaa blinked her eyes open and this time her vision was clear. She was in the very heart of her old home. The mighty *bolivar* trees, the standing spirits of Kamaalis long past, rose all around, protective and watchful, leaves whispering secrets amongst themselves as she remembered. Standing before the trees, the whole tribe surrounded her, dressed in the draping leaf-leather of green, gold and red. Their fine faces were filled with revulsion. They backed away as she sat up. Even her brother. She caught sight of another familiar face. Jaai. She and Jaai had been best friends as children. Rebaa looked to her with hope but Jaai's usually warm gaze was filled with only fear. She turned her beautiful face away, tears glistening in her dark purple eyes. Saddened, Rebaa staggered to her feet and nearly fell. She might be healed but she was still dangerously weak.

Sefaan reached out to steady her. "Get her some food," she commanded.

Nobody moved. Sefaan glared around at them all.

"No, Sefaan," this time Aardn's voice was firm. "You may have forced us to keep her here, but we will not help her or look after her. We will not anger Achala by aiding what she Herself forbade at the beginning of time. The Holy Creator is already leaving our people. I will not risk provoking her further." She stared around the group, her eyes lingering severely on Barias' tortured face. "Listen, all, I speak as your Elder. No one is to help the heretic or her Forbidden offspring. She must live on the fringes, unseen and ignored, unless one wishes to evoke the wroth of Achala Herself."

The tribe shrank further away from Rebaa and Sefaan, who still stood by her side. Rebaa gazed around at them. They who had once been her friends and family. Barias had his eyes fixed upon the baby in her arms. He might as well have been staring at a venomous snake. His scarred face was pale and agonised. Rebaa's face closed against him. Fine. She would do without him. As long as they let her keep her baby and stay under the protection of the tribe, that was all that mattered. She could do without any of them. She had learned to fend for herself.

Sefaan snorted derisively. "I guarantee that Achala has more important things on her mind. So be it," she said and pulled Rebaa away from the wall of prejudiced eyes. "Come, child."

Rebaa stumbled after the Kamaali woman as she lead her through the massive *bolivar* trees that her people called home. They stopped at the very edge of the mighty grove at the roots of one of the last red-gold sentinels.

"She will look after you," Sefaan said, staring up at the tree. Rebaa studied the *bolivar*. Unkempt and deserted, it was unoccupied and out of the way. Perfect. This would be hers. This would be where she raised her child by herself without any help from her people.

"Here," Sefaan said. The ancient woman held out a large root. Rebaa took it hungrily. Despite a bad taste, the gora root's flesh was the most nourishing food the Achalaja had to offer. No more meat, she realised in relief.

"I'll make you some clothes," the Kamaali continued, eyeing Rebaa's current attire with thinly veiled contempt. "There's no need for you to stand out any more than you need to."

"Thank you," Rebaa whispered, finally slipping back into her native tongue. She caught Sefaan's hand briefly. "Thank you for saving our lives." She would be forever in her debt. But she would not get too close. Never again. She would not put anyone else at risk for her mistakes. She must walk this forbidden path on her own now. She had survived. That was all that mattered. All else fell away. She looked down at her baby and smiled. He blinked at her, unaware of the commotion he had caused.

"The Great Spirit commanded," Sefaan said by way of explanation. "I will leave you alone now," the old one began to turn away. "Rest. They will not touch you. I have their promise. Just promise me that you will stay out of their way. Do nothing to provoke them. Especially Aardn."

Rebaa dipped her head in thanks once again. She started for the tree, holding her baby to her.

"Oh!" Sefaan called, turning back one last time. A smile played around the corners of her depthless eyes. "What are you going to call him?"

Rebaa blinked. In all that had happened since his birth, she had not even thought to bestow a name upon him. She peered down into his bright green eyes for a long moment and felt the strength of his spirit. Powerful even now. *Little strong one,* Nen's voice floated through her memory. She could almost see her friend there, black gaze warm and comforting, nodding her approval. She smiled gently.

Rebaa's eyes were enigmatic as they met Sefaan's. Wordlessly, she turned away and climbed up the abandoned tree that was to be her home from now on. She paused long enough to call back over her shoulder to the ancient one waiting below.

"His name is Juaan," she said and disappeared inside the living walls.

Epilogue

His mother was dead. The knowledge of that crushed Juaan's heart in an unforgiving fist. He collapsed to his knees on the ground at the base of the crumbling tree where he had lived with his mother for eight Furies. They had already taken her emaciated body away to Cast it to the river. They could not afford to attract sickness.

He had not been permitted to attend. He was an outcast. Forbidden. An object to be feared and mistrusted. He did not belong. Juaan gasped, clutching at his chest as another wave of grief and despair tore at him. His mother was the only one who had ever looked upon him without fear or contempt. She had been the very center of his belonging. Now she was gone and he did not belong anywhere anymore. The ties that had bound him had been severed and he was adrift. Lost. A Forbidden child amidst those who would prefer to see him dead.

They were the reason his mother was dead. They had not helped her. They had abandoned her. Anger burned hot beside his grief. He felt an uncontrollable energy building up inside him such as he'd never felt before. His fists clenched. Was this what it was supposed to feel like? Achala's Gift? He had always struggled to call upon it before. He bared his teeth as he gathered the energy to him.

"Juaan?" a soft voice called tentatively.

He snarled. It was not the voice he wanted to hear. His mother was dead and it was all because of them. All because of their hatred. It was *their* fault. All *his* fault for existing! It was everybody's fault! The world was a cruel, awful place. With a cry he lashed out with the energy that had been gathering within him. It exploded forth like an unstoppable gale, powerful and completely uncontrolled. Trees creaked and the younger ones shrivelled. A great commotion broke out as birds took to the air, shrieking in alarm. Somewhere in the distance, the wolves started to howl, made uneasy by the disruption he had caused. Spent, Juaan finally broke down and cried.

"Juaan?" Now the voice was wary, afraid.

He turned to glare at the speaker. What did they want now? Had they finally come to throw him to the elements? Finally strip him of what little protection they had offered?

It was Jaai who stood there. She waited just a few strides away. Her weight was shifted in a way that told him she was deliberating whether or not to flee from him - the abomination. He snorted and turned his reddened eyes away from her. Let her run. Of all the tribe, Jaai had been the most supportive of his mother. She had helped as much as the Elders' constraints had allowed her. She had avoided him as much as she could, of course, but she had been sympathetic to Rebaa's plight.

A fresh sob shook Juaan's body. Maybe if he just knelt here long enough, the Great Spirit would come and take him, too, and he could be reunited with his mother. Dimly, he was aware of a soft gasp and he realised Jaai was still standing there. When he met her eyes again, he saw that her wariness had been overcome with pity. She had been reading his emotions. He did not think anyone had ever done so before.

"You are just a boy, aren't you?" she whispered.

Juaan did not really know how to respond to that so he just stared at her helplessly. All the fight had gone out of him. Her eyes softened for a moment then hardened with determination. It seemed to Juaan that Jaai had come to a decision. She stepped forward quickly, her hand outstretched. Instinctively, Juaan flinched away.

"Don't be afraid, young one," Jaai spoke soothingly. "I won't hurt you. I made a promise to your mother. I am going to take care of you now."

Her words broadsided him. His thoughts buzzed without focus as Jaai's hand closed around his arm and pulled him to his feet. Young as he was, he was already as tall as Jaai. Juaan did not miss the flash of unease that crept back into the Achalaja woman's eyes.

"Achala, forgive me," he heard her murmur softly to herself. Her mouth was set in a grim line, however, and she continued to pull him firmly through the massive trees without hesitation.

"Jaai!" a male voice snapped from nearby. It was filled with consternation. "What are you doing with that?! Get away from it."

Juaan supposed he should feel angry or hurt by the words but he felt nothing. He did not care. He was beyond feeling now. Beside him, Jaai sighed resignedly but straightened her back, preparing to face her mate.

"We have got to take care of him now, Talaan."

Silence. Talaan stood as if waiting for his Joined One to reveal her vile deception and admit her true purpose. She did not. Jaai's firm gaze did not so much as flicker.

"Have you lost your mind?!" Talaan spat, finally recovering his senses enough to speak. Even Juaan could feel his outrage as it rolled out in waves. "He is Forbidden! His existence goes against the very will of Achala. Would you so curse our family?"

"He is just a boy, Talaan," Jaai replied resolutely. "I do not wish to anger the blessed Achala but I made a promise. Sefaan herself said we must care for him as our own. She told me it was essential and sent me to Rebaa before the Great Spirit took her." Jaai tightened her hold on Juaan's arm. "I will *not* go against the wisdom of the Last Kamaali. She who speaks for the Great Spirit himself. We must care for this boy. We have no choice. May Achala forgive us."

Talaan's lips thinned in anger and his fists clenched but he could not challenge her words. It was forbidden to go against the will of a Kamaali. He was caught between the two greatest edicts of his people. "This is madness," he raged helplessly. "I will have no part of it!"

Jaai shrugged. "That is your choice, Talaan. It is I who am bound, not you." With that she released Juaan's arm and bounded effortlessly into the nearest *bolivar* tree. Juaan stood, swaying on his feet, his eyes cast down to the black earth beneath his feet. He avoided making eye contact with the raging Talaan. He did not want to anger Jaai's mate further by sullying him with his accursed gaze after all.

After a few interminable moments, Jaai returned, climbing back down the great tree. She was carrying something. Talaan's rage spiked to a new level and he moved towards her in angry protest. One glare from Jaai stopped him in his tracks, the force of her will unassailable. "It is meant to be, Talaan," she whispered. "Do not interfere." Then, muttering a quick prayer, she placed the bundle that she carried on the ground between herself and Juaan.

Juaan blinked in mild surprise. The bundle was an infant. All wrapped up in cotton moss and leaves, she protested as her mother placed her on the ground. Her face was rumpled and disapproving. She obviously hadn't been ready to be roused from her nap. The light hurt her sleepy eyes. They were the deepest indigo.

"Nyri," Jaai spoke. "I want you to meet Juaan."

All sleepy protest fled. Juaan felt a strange thrill as the little girl met his gaze for a brief instant before ducking her head. He watched as she pushed herself clumsily onto her still unsure feet and totter away to hide behind her mother's legs. Juaan was surprised to feel a fresh stab of pain in his heart. He had thought he was beyond all feeling. So what if the child was afraid of him. Everybody was afraid of him. He should be used to it by now. And yet he felt this infant's rejection keenly. His eyes fixed upon that little girl as they had not focused upon anything or anyone since his mother's spirit had left him.

"Nyri," Jaai spoke gravely to her. "Juaan lost his mama last night. He is going to be a part of our family now. We have got to look after him because no one else will."

Talaan snorted and the girl looked to her father. A confused little frown wrinkled her brow. She did not respond to her mother's words.

"Nyri?" Jaai questioned. "Nyri." She gave her daughter a nudge with her heel. "Nyriaana!"

The words struck a chord in Juaan and before he even knew why he did it, he sang: "Nyri, Nyri, Nyriaana."

She giggled. The sound was like the soft bubbling of a brook. Indigo eyes peered out at him and reached right into his very soul. She crawled from behind her mother's legs to get a better look. Her gaze missed nothing and Juaan became keenly aware of just how strange he must appear to her. He felt like hiding himself away before the inevitable happened. He was tired of everyone's fear and mistrust. He wanted his mother. He wanted to be wrapped in her unconditional love. His grief rose, once again threatening to cripple him. But as he stared with increasingly blurring vision into the face of this child, he saw no fear there, merely innocent curiosity.

Her eyes widened in consternation when they settled upon his tear stained face. With a determined frown, the little girl pushed herself once more onto her unsteady legs. This time she came tottering towards him. Juaan was so stunned by this that he did not think to move out of her reach. By the time he recovered his wits, it was too late. She had him. Tiny arms reached around his legs and tightened in an embrace, seeking to comfort him.

"Hello, Juaan," she said in a soft, halting little voice. "Don' cry. I be your friend. Make it better?"

Juaan's voice choked off in a strangled sob as fresh tears came pouring down his face. The little girl's arms only tightened further. She could not know that they had reached right in to his soul and wrapped irrevocably around his heart. Binding him to her forever.

He sighed helplessly. "Hello, Nyri, Nyri, Nyriaana."

Coming Soon…

ANCESTORS

Book One of the Ancestors Saga

"The future is fast arriving. It sits in your hands… waiting."

Living deep in forgotten forests, the spiritual Achalaja race isolates itself from the rest of the world. Eight-year-old Nyriaana is an orphan of her tribe. Watched over by her friend and fellow orphan, Juaan, the pair are inseparable.

Tragically, Juaan is no true Achalaja. Tribal lore holds no place for a Forbidden child. As he grows closer to manhood, it is only a matter of time before the Elders cast him from the tribe; a death sentence in an unforgiving world. Blinded by innocence, Nyriaana has no idea that their days together are numbered.

When a cruel twist of fate tears everything she held dear apart, Nyriaana must choose between love and loyalty when survival may go against everything she was once taught to believe…

Sign up for the author's New Releases mailing list and get a free sneak peek at the prologue of *ANCESTORS,* the first novel in the Ancestors Saga.

Visit my website to continue your journey:

www.leholmes.com/ancestors-chapter-download

21747829R00059

Printed in Great Britain
by Amazon